"Okay, it takes t...

Sian glared at Leith and continued, "But the difference between us is that I had no idea I was participating in a one-night stand, and had I known, I wouldn't have."

Although her distaste of the affair had been rammed home, it was vital that he see her as an angry, wronged woman and not as some sniveling, brokenhearted female. "However, I'll recover. I'm not about to be enrolled in the ranks of your walking wounded!"

"You make it sound as though I've turned romance into some kind of blood sport," Leith protested. "I've always been honest in all my relationships."

"Which, translated, means that if some besotted female gets hurt, it's her tough luck," Sian taunted.

Leith's teeth ground together. "It means that the women I've dated have always known exactly what they were getting into."

ELIZABETH OLDFIELD began writing professionally as a teenager after taking a mail-order writing course, of all things. She later married a mining engineer, gave birth to a daughter and a son and happily put her writing career on hold. Her husband's work took them to Singapore for five years, where Elizabeth found romance novels and became hooked on the genre. Now she's a full-time writer in Scotland and has the best of both worlds—a rich family life and a career that fits the needs of her husband and children.

Books by Elizabeth Oldfield

HARLEQUIN PRESENTS
1132—CLOSE PROXIMITY
1212—SPARRING PARTNERS
1300—RENDEZVOUS IN RIO
1333—THE PRICE OF PASSION
1365—LOVE GAMBLE
1395—FLAWED HERO

Don't miss any of our special offers. Write to us at the following address for information on our newest releases.

Harlequin Reader Service
P.O. Box 1397, Buffalo, NY 14240
Canadian address: P.O. Box 603,
Fort Erie, Ont. L2A 5X3

ELIZABETH OLDFIELD

an accidental affair

Harlequin Books

TORONTO • NEW YORK • LONDON
AMSTERDAM • PARIS • SYDNEY • HAMBURG
STOCKHOLM • ATHENS • TOKYO • MILAN

Harlequin Presents first edition January 1992
ISBN 0-373-11429-X

Original hardcover edition published in 1990
by Mills & Boon Limited

AN ACCIDENTAL AFFAIR

CHAPTER ONE

SIAN stared across the desk. 'Leith Montgomery's off to Chile next week, but I won't be accompanying him?' she queried, her voice rising in surprise. 'Why not? We've worked together on his last three overseas assignments, so surely I should go along this time? I *expected* to go.'

'Sorry—Donald's been scheduled.'

Her brow puckered. 'But where's the sense in breaking up what you agreed was a winning combination?'

Alan Barnes, head of photography at the *Vulcan*, one of London's classier Sunday newspapers, gave an apologetic smile. 'Flexibility's the name of the game, and even if Donald does come over as a bit of a plodder, he is competent.'

'I'm not disputing that,' she replied, frowning through the glass partition to the hustle and bustle of the newsroom, where rows of computer screens flickered and people jabbered into telephones. 'What I am saying is——'

'Love-bird, the decision has been made.'

Sian swept from her chair, thrust her hands into the pockets of her khaki chinos, and glared. 'Well, I think it stinks!'

Startled, Alan sat back. Although he had heard that the *Vulcan*'s youngest and only female photographer possessed a propensity for speaking her mind, he had not witnessed it before. Neither had he met with any previous complaint. Other members of the team might grumble loudly and at mind-numbing length about what they saw as unfair designation of duties, but Sian Howarth never did. Whether the photo-opportunities she was allotted were trifling or important, all were accepted with cheerful good humour; which made her current dissatisfaction a disturbing change.

'The Chile job's nothing special,' he said, eager to restore harmony.

'If Leith's being despatched to handle it, no way can it be small potatoes,' Sian argued. 'He's the paper's star journalist.'

'And you're a star photographer,' Alan put in, at speed. 'Which means there'll be plenty of assignments for you here. Meaty ones.'

Her superior might have given a hasty compliment, yet he had spoken the truth. Despite her youth, a fusing of natural talent, intelligence and imagination had guaranteed Sian's rapid march to the leading edge of her discipline, and made her a valuable asset to the newspaper.

'But Leith and I have established a rapport,' she said, refusing to be placated.

A rapport? Lucky Leith, he thought, and felt a stab of envy. With her grape-green eyes, mane of pale flame-coloured hair and slim figure, Sian was, to quote the art critic's assessment, aesthetically pleasing to the eye—or, in more down to earth terms, a cracker. If he had been single, twenty years younger and—Alan sneaked a regretful look at his paunch—twenty pounds lighter, he would not be sitting on this side of his desk talking to her. No, sirree, he'd have been over there with arms outstretched, ready to console.

'A rapport?' he repeated, out loud. An idea abruptly hit and he leaned forward in agitation. 'Does that mean you've fallen for him?' He groaned. 'You've heard the girls gossiping about how Leith's dated some of the most delectable creatures around and, sooner or later, left every one of them flat? Sian, it was a warning! The guy might possess knockout charm, but he's also the nearest thing to a woman-eating panther on two legs. He snares 'em into what they fondly believe is a meaningful relationship, then without warning it's bang, finished, all over.' Alan sighed. 'I hate to tell you this, love-bird, but it'll be just the same with you. Leith may be hot-blooded, but that heart of his is cold. You get involved with him at your peril.'

Sian laughed. 'Don't panic. I'm not involved. I haven't fallen for him.'

'No?'

'No. I enjoy working with Leith, but our rapport is strictly business.'

The photography chief eyed her dubiously. 'His mix of English and Latin genes doesn't appeal? You do know the guy's a half-breed?'

'I realised he had to be something other than one hundred per cent Anglo-Saxon, but although we've talked about almost everything else under the sun somehow he's never mentioned his background.'

Alan folded his arms. 'Then allow me to fill you in. His father was Sir Charles Montgomery, merchant banker and Top Drawer gent—always fox-hunting with the county set or downing pink gins at some exclusive club, was old Charlie. He died last year. And Leith's mother was a breathtakingly beautiful heiress from foreign climes—Spain, I believe.'

'You're more of a gossip than all the girls here put together,' Sian teased. 'But, cross my heart, when I see him my knees do not wobble.'

'And Leith hasn't made any advances?' Alan enquired.

'None. I repeat, we have a purely professional relationship. He—well, I suppose you could say he treats me like a kid sister,' she said, then abruptly frowned.

This was the first time she had made a conscious definition, and hearing it voiced out loud made her wonder whether being regarded in such a way could be construed as wholly flattering. Certainly it was unusual. Most of the men she met took one look and proceeded to be anything but neutral!

'I guess Leith doesn't make advances, doesn't need to,' Alan observed. 'There might be a rapid turnover of women in his life, but they've probably all given him the wink. Oh, to be tall, dark and dynamic.'

Sian grinned. 'I can't imagine him playing footsie, can you? He has far too much style. He'd never——' She stopped dead. 'Did Giles Summerton have anything to do with my not going to Chile?' she demanded.

'I had to leave halfway, but I believe he did look in on the discussion. However——'

'I wish to have an audience with our political editor,' she interrupted, angry circles of colour beginning to burn in her cheeks.

Now she knew why she had been excluded from the South American assignment, and who was responsible! On her arrival at the *Vulcan*'s offices a year ago, the burly and bow-tied Mr Summerton had promptly noticed her and welcomed her. When regular enquiries as to how she was getting along had followed, Sian had been pleased. She was ambitious, and it would do her career no harm to keep on friendly terms and be visible. But over the months his interest had gradually dissipated into leers, oily compliments and sentences replete with sexual innuendo. Wary now, she had done her best to avoid him and had been alarmed when, in the middle of a progress meeting last week, the editor had suddenly marched into the room, grabbed a chair, and pushed in alongside. With legs spread wide so that his thigh had rubbed aggressively against hers, Giles Summerton had proceeded to ask questions and offer comments. Above the table, all had been proper, but below... He had pressed closer and, to her dismay, Sian had felt his stubby fingers creeping slowly and insidiously across her hip. She'd frozen. What to do? An aggrieved frown had been sent in his direction, but he had taken no notice. Her frown had intensified. Still the lecherous crawl had continued. Sitting up straight—and to hell with everyone realising the mischief he had been bent on—she had given a swift biff with her hand and knocked the offending paw away. Giles Summerton had not been pleased to have been publicly repulsed. Her lips compressed into a tight line. Neither was she pleased, *now*.

'Sorry, you can't see him,' Alan told her.

'Why not?' she demanded.

'Because he's taken the day off. I understand his wife insisted he have a blitz on the flower-beds.'

Sian felt deflated, but a moment later was forced to acknowledge that, courtesy of his gardening, she had been saved. Storming into the political editor's office to spell out that he was a SLUG in capital letters would have been insanely counter-productive. He would never allow her to bawl him out—and survive. So, she would have forfeited her job and the Chile assignment would have been lost forever.

Pushing her hands deeper into her pockets, Sian rocked back on her heels and smiled. The Chile trip had not disappeared down the tubes. Not yet. In his position of award-winning correspondent, Leith Montgomery possessed undeniable clout, so all it required was for *him* to advise Giles that *he* wanted her to go, that *he* needed her, and then ...

An impudent March wind snatched at the black chiffon which secured her hair. The knot loosened itself, the filmy scarf slipped, and for a split second seemed destined to go floating off over the South London rooftops. Sian grabbed. Hastily recapturing the red-gold strands which swirled around her shoulders, she bundled them up into a makeshift topknot. A tighter bow was tied, then, with her eyes swivelling to right and left, she continued along the cobbled backstreet. Although Leith had mentioned that he lived in a converted warehouse and she had noted down his address from the telephone book, her destination was proving elusive. Among the worn turn-of-the-century stone and brick buildings she saw a public house, a corner grocery store, a car repair workshop, but no sign of the private residence she required.

'Can I help you, luv?' a voice asked, and she turned to find that one of the motor mechanics had emerged to assist her.

'I'm looking for number forty-six,' Sian explained.

'You mean Leith.' He grinned, and after a few cheery observations about 'his old mate' the journalist, the articles he wrote, and the weather, the mechanic directed her across the road and down a flagged alley.

Halfway along a flight of steps led to a first-floor porch, so Sian climbed them and rang the bell. Footsteps sounded, the door opened and a dark-haired man wearing a black suit, the cuffs of the jacket rolled back over a billowy, open-necked white shirt, looked out.

She shone a wide smile. 'Good afternoon.'

His response was an impromptu stiffening, a narrowing of brown eyes, and, finally, a frown. 'Hi,' he said curtly.

Sian's sense of purpose faltered. Patience had never been one of her virtues and, desperate to resolve the issue, she had dashed out of the office and come straight here. Now her haste and lack of thought were regretted. The journalist invariably played classical music as an aid to concentration, and behind him strains of a symphony were flooding the air. Her smile flickered like a faulty neon sign. He was writing and she was intruding. Instead of this invasion of his privacy, she could—she should—have waited and spoken to him at work tomorrow.

'I'm sorry if I've disturbed you,' she apologised quickly, 'but I didn't——'

Leith Montgomery raised a long hand with square-tipped fingers. 'Give me ten minutes. There are a couple more paragraphs which I need to get down and then I'll be with you.' Showing her into a vast open-plan area, he nodded tersely towards a deep-cushioned cream leather sofa. 'Grab a pew.'

Sian sat down and, as her colleague returned to his labours, she gazed around. The only clue that his home had originally been built to store goods was in its size. Now floored in polished cherrywood and with huge windows and skylights, the airy expanse had been cleverly arranged to encompass the multifarious demands of modern life. Where she waited an oval Persian carpet formed the focus, and back from it stood cider-coloured units, one housing a music centre and television, another which acted as drinks cabinet, and a third where copper and pewter mugs were displayed. There was a hexagonal smoked-glass table and plenty of leafy potted plants. Looking further, she saw an elegant dining section and, beyond it, glimpsed a breakfast bar which marked the boundary of a sleek white kitchen. Sian turned to the other end of the floor, where a staircase led to a banistered gallery with doors off into what must have been two bedrooms.

'Almost through,' Leith muttered, and her eyes were drawn to the study nodule.

In the angle made by one wall of low bookshelves and another comprising filing cabinets stood a large desk bearing a computer, at the keyboard of which her colleague was typing with his customary electric pace. Sian examined him. Now that she had been told Latin blood ran in his veins, it seemed obvious. His thick, wavy hair, dark eyes and tawny skin declared his heritage, but there was more. She recalled how he made generous use of his hands when explaining a point, the effortless and understated theatricality of how he dressed, the proud, almost arrogant, certainty which said here was a man who could look after himself. And what about his English ancestry? Did that provide his dedication to the work ethic, his calm control, his sharp sense of humour? She nibbled pensively at her lip. Alan had been wrong about his having charm. Charm was too practised, too smooth. Instead, Leith Montgomery possessed that quality which was difficult to describe and equally difficult to miss—charisma. It meant he was positive, interesting and very nice to know.

'Cracked it,' he said suddenly, and grinned across at her.

Sian flushed, aware she had been caught staring. 'Er—that was the final draft?'

'All complete,' he confirmed. He came over to the compact-disc player and switched off the music. 'Fancy a cup of coffee?' he asked.

She smiled, understanding her interruption had been forgiven. 'Love one.'

'Black, two sugars?'

'Correct,' Sian replied, pleased he had remembered. He jerked his head, and she followed him into the kitchen. 'I like your house,' she said, as he plugged in a percolator and set out mugs.

'Thanks.' There was an amused arch of a brow. 'What do you think of the location?'

'I like that, too. It's a bit . . . down-at-heel, but it's cosy and the people seem friendly.'

'They are. There's a great community spirit.' Leith rested a hip against a gleaming white unit. 'But you should have heard my father's reaction. For a start, he reckoned that no one of any consequence ever lived south of the river, and when he discovered the neighbourhood I'd chosen he damn near threw a fit. He didn't approve of me doing the place up myself, either.'

Sian's green eyes opened wide. 'You did all this?'

'With my own fair hands. I didn't do everything,' he adjusted. 'The electrics and plumbing were beyond me, but I designed the interior, installed the windows, did the carpentry, which included laying the floor.'

'Wow!' she said in admiration and surprise.

Leith always looked urbane, as though his fingernails had never been dirty in his life, so it was difficult to imagine him sawing up planks or on his knees as he hammered. Or was it? Everyone had a multitude of faces and the only one she had seen was that of the journalist. As the coffee began to perk, Sian smiled. Barging in might have been a trifle rash, but this view of him at home was opening up new and intriguing perceptions.

'So, smarty-pants, why the visit?' he enquired.

She took a breath. 'I wonder if you could find it in your heart to do me a favour?'

'I'll try.'

'It's Chile. I understand Donald's been written in to accompany you, but that's not fair. I'm the one who should go.'

Leith lifted the bubbling percolator and poured out two mugs of coffee. 'Why?' he queried.

'Isn't it obvious? Because we're a team.'

'Are we?'

Sian frowned. This was not the response she had anticipated. 'We've done three jobs together, and you did say you wanted me with you on the next,' she reminded him. 'You also said you'd make sure it happened.'

'Maybe,' Leith began, 'but——'

'You told me the pictures I took in Washington were worth a thousand of your painfully polished words. You reckoned they complemented your text far better than anyone else's had ever done!'

'They did.'

'So please will you pass on the information to Giles Summerton?' Sian appealed.

'Giles?'

She nodded. 'Would you tell him how important it is that I partner you.'

Leith handed her a brimming mug. 'It isn't important.'

'It is—to me, at least!' she protested, disgruntled to find that, instead of providing tub-thumping support, for some reason he was being apathetic. Sian went with him back to the sofa. 'If I'm dropped for no apparent cause, people will decide it must be because my work wasn't good enough and that in some way I'm lacking.'

'No.'

'*Yes*. And it's not only at the *Vulcan* that there'll be doubts. The London newspaper fraternity is close-knit and rumours hurtle around, so before you know it folk on other papers will have downgraded me, too. Then, if

I should want to leave the *Vulcan* some time,
I'll be in schtum.'

Leith sampled his coffee. 'You're
exaggerating.'

Vigorously she shook her head. 'Working
with you has given me a high profile—and
kudos, for which I'm grateful. But I've helped
you, too,' Sian went on, when there was no
reply. 'Who was it who was told that the rebel
commander you were desperate to talk to in
Afghanistan paid visits to a woman in the next
village, and who discovered the name of the
favourite bar of that drug dealer in
Washington?'

He sighed. 'You. You're a whizz at being
adopted by strangers, and you have a nose like
an ant-eater when it comes to wheedling out
secrets,' he said drily.

'Which means that, for both our sakes, I
should travel to Chile.'

Leith took another mouthful. 'You don't let
go easy, do you? Sian, there'll be other overseas
assignments, I promise.'

'You promised me this one and look what's
happened,' she retaliated.

'The time after when I fly off into the wide
blue yonder you'll be strapped in the seat beside
me, scout's honour.'

She wavered. Should she settle for his assurance? Dared she? But if Giles Summerton
successfully banned her from the Chile oper-

ation, a precedent would be set which might not augur well for the future. Would her chances of being selected for the international jobs—the status jobs—suddenly wither? Was she going to be eliminated from photographing topical places and topical events? Could she find herself hanging endlessly around outside night-clubs waiting for celebrities to appear—as a member of the paparazzi?

'I'm not interested in next time, I'm interested in now,' Sian announced, her chin jutting. 'So would you kindly instruct our beloved political editor to rescind his peevish veto and——?'

Leith's head jerked round. 'Giles's veto?' he queried. At that moment the doorbell pealed. 'Back in a minute,' he mumbled and, relinquishing his mug, he strode off to answer it.

As Sian drank her coffee, she frowned. She did not understand his reluctance to help. It was most annoying and disappointing—it almost smacked of treachery. When he returned, she would remind him again of how well they operated in tandem. Neither Afghanistan, Washington nor West Germany, for that matter—a terrorist bomb had been the *raison d'être* there—had been easy assignments, yet they had plunged in, sparking ideas off each other and being mutually stimulated. Working together had given them both a buzz, and, against all odds, they had also had *fun*. She would remind him of that, too.

'I've called to see if you'd like me to do your ironing—or maybe some cleaning?' a woman said breathlessly, as Leith opened the door.

'No, thanks.'

'I'm perfectly willing.'

'Sorry, it isn't convenient.'

'I finished work early on purpose.'

His voice hardened. 'Not today, Caroline.'

Sian had assumed his visitor to be some kind of home help, but when she glanced through the arch which opened on to the hall she saw a willowy chignoned blonde in her early thirties. Clad in an immaculate salmon-pink suit and with flawless make-up, she looked like the kind of woman who could travel in an open sports car without getting a single hair out of place. How sickening. Abruptly reminded of her own windswept state, Sian pushed a straggle of red-gold from her brow. And Miss Perfect was begging to do Leith's housework? She cringed. It could only be the ploy of a discarded woman desperate to wriggle her way back into his affections.

'What about tomorrow?' the blonde appealed.

He shook his head. 'If you must come, make it Sunday.'

'Tim suggested we visit friends at the coast on Sunday,' she said doubtfully, but then she smiled. 'I'll cancel.'

Leith gave a careless shrug. 'Up to you.'

As though expecting more, and certainly *wanting* more, Caroline hovered, but he stood as silent and unrelenting as an Easter Island statue.

'Till Sunday, then,' she murmured, with such reluctance that Sian felt a pang of sympathy. The blonde's adoration of Leith was plain and, even though his attitude said the feeling was not reciprocated, it would not have hurt him to be a little more amiable.

'Sunday,' he agreed.

'Bye, bye,' his visitor trilled. She was turning to leave when suddenly she glanced beyond him and caught sight of Sian. Like a soufflé collapsing, her face fell. 'I didn't realise you had . . . company,' she said awkwardly.

Sian gave a glassy smile. There was no need to be told that 'company' meant she had been installed in the woman's mind as Leith's lover.

'This is Sian Howarth. She's a photographer at the *Vulcan* and from time to time we work together,' her host explained, with unconcealed impatience. 'She called to discuss a business matter.'

Caroline's brow crinkled and, as though she would later be awarding marks, her gaze made a slow journey from the top of Sian's dishevelled head to her feet. When her inspection was complete, her face cleared and she bestowed a condescending smile. 'I should have guessed,' she said.

Sian bristled. She did not appreciate being dismissed in such a derogatory manner. As a 'monkey'—newspaper jargon for photographers because they were reckoned to spend a lot of their time up trees—her working uniform consisted of T-shirt and cotton chinos, a tan suede jacket resplendent with zips, and cowboy boots. Maybe she was not as fashionable as she could be, and admittedly nowhere as chic as the blonde, yet she resented the idea that her appearance automatically disqualified her from being regarded as Leith Montgomery's girlfriend. Two for effort and zero for style, she thought indignantly. Thanks a lot!

Glancing down, she frowned at her faded and somewhat threadbare trousers. Leith sometimes called her 'smarty-pants', which she had blithely assumed to be a term of casual affection, but now it struck her that he could be being casually sarcastic instead.

'Goodbye, Caroline,' Leith said firmly.

His visitor wiggled her fingers. 'Cheerio.'

'That's my shirts ironed for going to Chile,' he grinned as he closed the door.

Sian looked at him. 'You mean you asked her to come on Sunday because——?'

'Because I'm flying Monday and need to have my clothes ready,' he completed, striding back to retrieve his coffee.

'But Caroline was planning to go out,' she protested.

'So?'

In rapid succession Sian had felt sorry for the blonde, disliked her, and now the bond of female kinship against the manipulative male was evoked.

'So you deliberately used her!' Her green eyes glittered. 'I think that's despicable!'

Leith drained his mug in one gulp. 'I reckon it's practical,' he drawled.

She glowered. On being regaled with the exotica which seemed to surround any good-looking bachelor, Sian had promptly dismissed the 'love 'em and leave 'em' tales as much fiction based on minuscule fact. After all, she had never found Leith to be anything but agreeable, considerate and friendly. Yet wasn't today's treatment of Caroline evidence of a cold heart? And how had he treated the poor woman in the past?

'I suppose you claimed you were being *practical*,' she demanded, 'when you ditched her?'

'Ditched her? I haven't,' he protested.

'Caroline wasn't your——?'

'Mistress?' he enquired drily, when she hesitated. 'No. Sorry to disappoint, but Caroline and I have never been, and never will be, what is commonly termed "an item".'

Sian's attack crumbled into dust. 'Oh,' she said lamely.

'And as for the accusation that I'm using her, she's also using me—to try and make her boyfriend, Tim, jealous and thus, hopefully, propose.'

'But she fancies you,' Sian countered.

'She fancies any man who's single,' Leith retorted. 'Let me explain. Caroline is the daughter of some friends of my father. She heard I'd bought this place and soon after I moved in she called, found me up to my ankles in sawdust, and kindly offered to clean it up. Astonishing as it may seem, she actually does get a kick out of doing that kind of thing. I was grateful, and when she appeared and proceeded to repeat the performance the following week I was grateful again. She came by on so many subsequent occasions that it became necessary to find some way to thank her, and so I decided to take her out for a slap-up meal. But that's all it was, straight thanks.' He arched a brow. 'I did not deflower her between the hors-d'oeuvre and the fish course.'

Sian ignored his jibe. 'Yet she became infatuated?' she demanded.

The sculptured curve of his mouth turned down at the corners. 'I suspect the evening out prompted her to wonder whether I might be an easier fish to land than slippery Tim, though the only reason I'd marry someone is if they got me pregnant,' Leith said sardonically. 'However, since then never a week has passed by without Caroline visiting me.'

Silence.

'Couldn't it be your presence in the background which is keeping Tim from popping the question?' Sian suggested.

He frowned, considering what she had said. 'It's a theory,' he concurred.

'So why not inform Caroline you don't need her to do your housework and give him a chance?'

'What happens to my shirts?'

'You either iron the damn things yourself or send them to the laundry!'

Leith made a face. 'I suppose I could.'

'In my opinion, it's not "could", it's *"should"*!'

Her conviction seemed to hit home.

'Right,' he agreed, 'when I get back from Chile I'll tell Caroline I can manage on my own.'

Sian favoured him with a long smile which lit up her entire face. 'About Chile,' she started. 'I——'

'There's something I must explain,' he broke in. 'Giles Summerton had nothing to do with your not joining me. It was my decision.'

'Yours?' His declaration snatched the air from her lungs. 'But—but I thought we were friends,' she stammered, as the realisation and its ramifications began to sink in. 'We *were* friends. You said I'd be with you on your next trip. You——'

'Now don't get all bent out of shape,' Leith protested, waving his hands around as though he were conducting an orchestra. 'It's just that I never realised then that I'd be going to Chile.'

'What difference does that make?'

'It could be dangerous.'

'You've spent time there?' Sian demanded. 'You have first-hand experience?'

'No-o,' he admitted.

'But Chile's more dangerous than Afghanistan or the slums of Washington at night? Cut it out,' she said scornfully.

'Latin America is a volatile continent,' Leith proclaimed, his hands swooping up and down. 'People have been known to disappear from the streets, never to be seen again. Dictators operate hit-gangs. There are frequent violations of human rights.'

'Listen, I have a friend whose father works for a British company in Santiago and she visits her parents at least once a year. She's never run into any trouble and neither have her folks.'

'Are they newspaper photographers?' he demanded, and smartly answered his own question. 'Negative.'

'You reckon that makes me vulnerable?' Sian protested, her disbelief rampant. 'I've been within close range of gunfire and lived to tell the tale. I've mixed with the mêlée and——'

'OK, OK,' Leith cut in, 'you're a tough butterfly.'

'One who knows that being brave can equate with being dead. Like you, I don't go in for heroics. In fact, given the chance I'm the first under the table. However, I am willing to accept whatever risks exist in Chile.'

'You may be, but I'm not,' he said firmly, 'and so you're not coming with me.'

'I——'

'My mind's made up!'

Sian's stomach cramped. She felt let down. Sold out. Deserted. His claim of danger—and saving her from it—did not ring true. The brutal fact was that he did not want her with him. So much for friendship! So much for the happy highs which she had been so certain existed! His pleasure in her company had been a trick of the light. To her dismay, she felt her throat begin to thicken. Sian swallowed hard. It was ridiculous to feel so broken up and would be humiliating to cry.

'South American photographs would have greatly enhanced my portfolio,' she burst out, in an explosion of confused anger. 'However, if you're determined to stop me——'

'It's for your own good,' Leith said heavily.

'My own good? Huh! I——'

'If the screaming harridan from hell is about to unload another earful she needn't bother, because it'll change nothing.' He sliced a hand. 'Zilch.'

Red-gold head held high, Sian rose from the sofa. 'Thank you for the coffee. Thanks for everything!' she snarled, and she marched from the apartment, slamming the door behind her.

Late Sunday evening the telephone rang.

'For you, Sian,' her father called upstairs. 'It's Alan Barnes.'

'Hope I haven't disturbed your beauty sleep,' the photography chief apologised when she greeted him, 'but we're in a bit of a fix. It's Donald. His wife's just phoned to say he's been carted off to hospital with acute food poisoning.' There was a pause. 'I don't suppose you could pack a bag, put a film in your camera, and be at Heathrow by nine a.m. tomorrow?'

'Ready to check in for the flight to Chile?'

'Please.'

Sian's mouth spread into a seraphic smile. 'You can rely on me,' she said.

CHAPTER TWO

THEY had crossed ocean and jungle, cities and vast grassy plains, and now the jumbo jet had reached the snow-covered mountains of the Andes. On this, the final leg of their journey, they were, so the pilot had recently announced, cruising close to Aconcagua which, at almost twenty-three thousand feet, was the highest peak in the entire four-and-a-half-thousand-mile-long range. Spellbound, Sian gazed out of the window. Not so far below lay a bleak and frozen world. A world of jagged pinnacles and majestic crags, of treacherous blinding-white plateaus. A world where few humans had ever trod and fewer still survived. Whimsically she smiled, contrasting nature's hostile splendour with the man-made comfort from which she viewed it. A cushion was at her back, a blanket covered her knees, and in her hand she held a glass of white wine—a prelude to the luncheon which would shortly be served.

'Awe-inspiring,' Leith muttered, craning forward beside her. 'To coin an *un*inspired description.'

'But it is. Poor Donald, having to miss all this.'

He gave her an old-fashioned look. 'Makes you want to weep, doesn't it. You're sure you can't remember slipping him that mouldy cheese?'

Sian sighed. 'OK, having me around doesn't fit into your scheme of things, but I'm here to do a job. Period. I won't be a nuisance. And if you're worried about having to translate everything on my behalf, you needn't be. For several years I've spent holidays at my parents' timeshare in Marbella, so although I can't claim to be fluent I do have sufficient Spanish to get by.'

'Whereas I don't.'

Her brows rose. 'You don't speak Spanish?'

'Not a word.'

'Oh, I assumed that with your mother——'

Leith shot her a steely glance. 'What do you know about my mother?' he demanded.

Sian's cheeks burned. 'Nothing. Nothing at all.' She made a vague gesture. 'Someone happened to mention she came from Spain.'

'In other words, you were discussing me,' he said brusquely. 'Well, just remember that the grapevine is notorious for not getting its facts straight.'

Her hot face went hotter. This, she assumed, would be a reference to the rumours which had attached themselves to his love life.

'I will,' Sian promised.

Leith took a mouthful of gin and tonic. 'You aren't aware that my mother walked out on my father and me when I was seven?' he enquired.

'No,' she replied, surprised to find him now prepared to talk about something which, with hindsight, it was obvious he had kept firmly locked away.

'When I say "walked out" that's exactly what happened.' He frowned down into his drink. 'I'd just begun my first term as a boarder at prep school when she decided to return from whence she came, but there were no fond fare-wells, no tearful note to her son, not even a phone call to warn I was about to be abandoned. She simply upped and went.'

Sian heard a wealth of bitterness in his voice.

'Why did she go?' she asked. 'Without saying goodbye, I mean.'

Leith moved a shoulder. 'No idea.'

'She hasn't told you?'

'I haven't heard from her since.'

Aghast, she looked at him. 'Never?'

'Never ever.'

Sian brooded over what he had said. Her own family was close-knit and stable, which made it difficult to comprehend the way-wardness of others. But how could any woman turn her back on her child, and continue to keep it turned?

'Surely your father must have explained her reasons?' she said.

He shook his head. 'After my mother left so abruptly he refused to speak about her.' Leith swirled the liquid in his glass. 'I'd been homesick at school—as an only child I hated being uprooted—so to arrive back and find that not only had she vanished, but also that my father had declared her a forbidden sub- ject——' he took a swift mouthful '—it was difficult.'

'And you still miss her?' Sian asked, thinking that this could explain the occasional 'haunted' quality which she had detected in his make-up.

Leith scowled as though resenting her per- ception, but then he relented. 'Her departure's always been a sorrow,' he agreed. 'My father was a strict authoritarian and as a small boy I was frightened of him, so to be without my mother was...appalling. Throughout my childhood and increasingly so in my ado- lescence I tried to discover why she'd felt it necessary to make such a final exit,' he went on, 'but my father always recognised what I was working up to and side-stepped. Matters came to a head in my early twenties. By then I'd reached the state where knowing had become something of an obsession, so I chose an evening when we were alone and tackled him.'

'And?' she prompted, when he frowned.

'He accused me of picking at a scab which should have been allowed to heal long ago and became very uptight, very aggressive, almost apoplectic. My father had already been diagnosed as suffering from a heart condition—it was a coronary which eventually killed him—and, as I didn't want him collapsing at my feet, I saw no option but to withdraw. That was the last time I broached the subject.' Leith sighed. 'I've never been able to understand how my mother could be so callous. She seemed such a gentle, caring person——' he shrugged '—though I guess kids don't have too much in the way of judgement. It's ironical,' he continued, 'but I once overheard a conversation in which she vowed I still needed a mother's care and was far too young to be sent away to school, while my father insisted that if I was to be a success it was the only kind of education. She changed her mind about my needing her pretty damn quick,' he observed bitingly.

Sian winced. For all his friendly manner, Leith was not the kind of man who made it easy to see inside him and what she glimpsed now distressed her. 'But you are a success,' she said, needing to comfort.

'Not in my father's estimation,' he replied. 'Charles didn't rate being a "hack", as he called it, too highly. He'd far rather I'd gone into something Establishment and City, like him.'

'What a whacko!' she exclaimed.

Leith grinned. 'That's what I've always thought.'

'So your parents were divorced?' He nodded. 'And did your father marry again?'

'Yes; a couple of years after my mother skipped it he met Dorothy.'

'Did she take you under her wing?' Sian enquired.

A hand was tipped from side to side in a 'so-so' gesture. 'Dot's always preferred acting the hostess with the mostest to being the devoted stepmother, but we rubbed along OK, and still do.' He frowned. 'I spent the weekend with her a couple of weeks ago.'

'Doesn't she know why your mother departed?'

Leith shook his head. 'My father became agitated when Dot asked questions, too.'

'Perhaps she left him for another man and he found the hurt too much to handle?' Sian mused.

'Maybe, or perhaps she preferred the luxury lifestyle her family could provide. My father was a long way from poor, yet in comparison he might have seemed so. Why am I telling you all this?' he demanded abruptly.

She grinned. 'Because you want to?'

'Or because you seem to encourage the yielding up of secrets and I've been on this plane so damn long my defences have crumbled,' he remarked, his dark brows coming down.

'Your family history is a secret?'

'No, but—you're looking very classy,' Leith said, in a blunt change of subject.

'Thanks.'

The one positive result of her visit to his home had been a determined Saturday shopping spree. This, fortuitously, had enabled her to pack her suitcase with a couple of new outfits and to arrive at the airport wearing a square-shouldered pewter and white striped jacket, white silk shirt and pale grey slacks. Her feet were clad in grey court shoes, while on her head had been an emerald-green trilby. As she had walked through the departures hall, heads had turned and admiring glances had come from all directions. Only the creased and bulky black leather camera bag which had hung from her shoulder had indicated that this elegant young woman was, in reality, a working girl.

'The hat's a killer.' Leith smiled, casting a look up at the luggage rack where her trilby had been reverently stored.

'Makes a change,' Sian said, acting blasé.

This was the first time she could remember him acknowledging her appearance, let alone praising it, and, even if their alliance was not the friendship she had once imagined, his compliments still tasted sweet. Yet she had no intention of allowing him to discern her pleasure.

'As far as the language is concerned,' Leith went on, in another abrupt switch of topic, 'Adriana Sanchez has arranged an interpreter, so a Raul someone-or-other will be waiting when we land. He'll drive us around and interpret for the two weeks we're there.'

'Who's Adriana Sanchez?' Sian enquired.

'I'm sorry, I assumed you'd have come across her when she visited the *Vulcan* offices last year, but it must have been before you arrived. She's a Chilean freelance from whom we buy linage from time to time,' Leith explained. 'A very pretty woman.'

'She's the one who warned you Santiago was a snake pit for photographers?' Sian could not resist saying archly, but before he could reply she hurried on. 'After Alan called I rang my friend and asked her to tell me more about the place. Jill said that, while admittedly there are spasmodic riots, the only alarm she's ever felt was at the time of a slight earth tremor.' She paused, recalling her conviction that if he had been sent to Chile the assignment could not be insignificant. 'You specialise in crises of various kinds, so it occurred to me that you may have picked up murmurings of a government *coup* and Giles has despatched you to cover it. In that case if we happened to be in the wrong place at the wrong time it could get a little scary,' she conceded, 'but——'

'A *coup*?' He gave a grunt of surprise. 'If one's being planned it's the first I've heard.'

'It is?' Sian frowned. 'So why——?'

'My purpose in visiting the country is to gather material for a series of articles which will discuss Chile's place in the global fraternity,' Leith told her, a touch impatiently. 'Arrangements have been made through the Chilean embassy for me to interview a couple of government ministers, but I also intend to speak to people from the various strata of society—and I need you to photograph them against the background of the neighbourhoods in which they live. Plus take shots of anything else of interest.'

She nodded. 'Alan explained.' Reaching into her bag, Sian pulled out her diary. 'I don't know if this is of any help, but Jill gave me the names of a couple of poor districts and two high-class ones.' She riffled through the pages. 'The poor areas are Peñalolén and Conchali, while——'

'Conchali?' Leith cut in. 'That isn't poor. You've got them the wrong way around.'

Her brow furrowed. She had taken a careful note of the information. 'Have I?' she said doubtfully.

'Yes, but just forget about Conchali and the rest,' he said, sounding irritated, 'and remember that *I'm* the one who runs the show around here.'

Sian gave a jokey salute. 'Yes, boss.'

*   *   *

Sprawled in a valley with the snow-clad foothills of the Andes forming a picture-postcard backdrop, Santiago was an enchanting city. Although the interpreter warned that the smog often hung low, today the air sparkled like crystal, the sun shone and the sky was blue. Here in the southern hemisphere autumn had painted its vivid colours, and the light breeze which stirred in the trees sent leaves of bronze and yellow and scarlet shimmering down to decorate the pavements of the broad avenues.

'Although I've seen photographs and heard descriptions, the European *feel* to the place still surprises me,' Leith commented, as they drove through plazas where fountains splashed, past churches rich with rococo embellishments, alongside beautiful parks.

'But Europe is responsible for most of our heritage. Indeed, it was a Spaniard who originally founded Santiago in 1541,' the interpreter told him.

Raul Villalobos was a short, dapper middle-aged man, with a bushy moustache and a bald spot cajoled into near invisibility. He had welcomed them with fervent *saludos* and given smiling assurances that not only was he happy to translate, but he would be delighted to answer all their questions.

'What was the Spaniard's name?' Leith asked.

'Pedro de Valdivia.'

'And exactly who was he?'

From her seat in the back of the car, Sian sent the Chilean a sympathetic glance. When he had offered to answer *all* questions, he could not have guessed he was destined to spend the next hour being relentlessly interrogated. Her gaze swung to Leith's dark head. On their other trips his journalist's mind meant he had always had an armoury of questions at the ready, yet he had never fired off so many so soon. They had not left the airport terminal before his bombardment had begun. He had, he'd informed Raul, done a fair amount of research, but he wanted to know more about the Chilean way of life. It turned out to be much, much more. Information was demanded about the social structure, the apportionment of wealth, the patriotism of the people, on and on, and now he was quizzing Raul about the country's past. As he had said that ten years or so ago he had been obsessed with knowing about his mother, now he seemed equally obsessed with knowing about Chile.

Sian eyed him curiously. Beneath this thirst for knowledge she had detected a tension, one which, on reflection, had been evident at Heathrow and which had increased in line with their flying time. Although she knew her presence rankled, she found it hard to believe it could wind him up so tight, so what was responsible? Had the long hours of travelling frayed his nerves? Were thoughts of the work he needed to accomplish in the next fourteen days troubling him? Neither travel nor work had been a worry before, but now Leith was on edge and volubly intense. As they drove along his questions kept shooting out—who did this? Why? What happened next?—until Raul began to look quite battered.

'You have unusual hair,' the interpreter declared, attempting a diversion when his cross-examiner paused for breath. He smiled at Sian through the rear-view mirror. 'No one has such a colour in Chile.'

Hooking an arm along the back of his seat, Leith turned to eye the curtain of burnished flame which curled loosely around her shoulders. 'You don't get it so often anywhere,' he remarked.

'Lovely,' Raul murmured, 'so very, very lovely. Yes?' he said, looking to the younger man for agreement, but Leith sat forward.

'What's the situation with protests and mass demonstrations?' he enquired.

Sian fixed the back of his head with a stun-gun glare. Damn his questions! Damn him! He could have said yes. He could at least have nodded. It wouldn't have cost him anything. But, it seemed, his compliments started and ended with her clothes.

The grilling once more in full swing, their journey continued. For a while Sian listened, but in time her eyelids began to droop. Although she had slept on the plane the rest had been fitful, and now weariness was stealing over her. Their surroundings grew hazy, the voices of the two men blurred. As they joined the stop-wait-go of the city-centre traffic, she was dimly aware of Raul saying they would soon be at their accommodation. It was located in an excellent area, with a shopping mall nearby, and a cinema, and many fine restaurants, and ... Sian fell asleep.

'Soon' might have been five minutes or ten or twenty; whichever, it seemed like seconds, for the next thing she knew the car had stopped, the engine noise had ceased, and Raul was holding wide her door. Blinking herself awake, she collected up her hat, hooked her camera bag over her shoulder and went with her companions into the lobby of a modern tower block. A uniformed porter was sitting at a desk, and she watched in a daze as he handed over keys and some verbal information.

'You are up high, on the twelfth floor.' Raul smiled.

A fast-speed lift delivered them to a private landing, where Leith unlocked a door. When their luggage had been placed inside, arrangements were made for the following day and, with another admiring glance at Sian's hair, the interpreter departed.

Walking into the room, Sian gazed around, and then swiftly thought back to the downstairs lobby. There had been no to and fro of guests, no lounges, no bar, no coffee shop. 'This isn't a hotel,' she said in a surprised voice.

'Don't miss a trick, do you, smarty-pants?' Leith remarked. 'It's an apart-hotel, where apartments are rented out on a weekly or monthly basis. It's a darn sight cheaper than a hotel and, as the woman who fixes travel at the *Vulcan* has been ordered to economise, this is what she came up with.' He shrugged. 'Looks fine to me.'

The beige-carpeted living-room was anonymously furnished, but a wall of windows which overlooked a golf course far below made it light and airy. A bitter-orange settee and chairs were set in a semi-circle before a wall-mounted television, and there was a small bar. To the left a table and long sideboard comprised the dining area, while in an alcove, half hidden behind a folding screen, she saw a compact kitchen.

'We're . . . both staying here?' Sian ventured.

'As the apartments are two-bedroomed, it would hardly be economical if we each had one. Though, of course, the accommodation was arranged in the expectation that it'd be Donald who accompanied me,' Leith pointed out astringently. He rubbed a tired hand across his brow. 'You don't object to sharing?' he demanded, as though her 'yes' would mean endless phone calls or even a deathly plod around Santiago, searching for a hotel room.

Sian gave a trill of laughter. 'Of course not. Men and women live together in flats. Strangers. And they don't——'

Aware of making an idiot of herself, she shut up. There was no need to justify the arrangement, nor to air any sexual connotations. Leith might not want it this way, but clearly he did not see anything untoward in their cohabiting—and she would be as casual as he.

'One bedroom,' Sian announced, walking across to peer into a double-bedded room furnished in toffee and cream. She opened a second door. 'Another one here. Identical.'

'But no *en suite* bathrooms, just one between us,' he remarked, as he came to make an inspection.

'Doesn't bother me,' she declared, being gloriously offhand.

'Nor me, so long as you don't leave long hairs in the shower,' Leith warned drolly. He went over to the kitchen alcove and drew back the screen. 'According to Raul, we're supposed to have been provided with a box of basic groceries. Yes, here it is. What I suggest we do is unpack, grab a bite to eat, then hit the sack. It may be early evening, but our body clocks are ticking away in the mid-hours of the night.'

He yawned. 'I feel as if I could sleep for a week.'

'Me, too. What time are we due out in the morning?'

'We're not. Raul's coming at two. I thought we needed a lie-in if we were to function properly in the afternoon. That's when I'm due to meet the politicians. Now, which bedroom would you like?'

Not much later, Sian's belongings were installed in the fitted wardrobe and drawers. Closing her suitcase, she went across to the kitchen. Among the groceries were rashers of bacon, tomatoes, and a carton of eggs, so, after making shouted enquiries to Leith who had yet to reappear, she started on dinner.

'Thanks, that was good,' he said with a smile when the food had been eaten and cups of coffee drunk. He stretched tiredly. 'It's been an age since anyone cooked a meal for me. However, the next time we eat in it's my turn. Lower your eyebrows, please. I might be a klutz with an iron, but I work wonders with fillet steak.'

'In other words, a creased shirt is neither here nor there, but there's no way you're going to starve to death?' Sian enquired pertly.

He grinned. 'Priorities are priorities.'

'How do you rate at drying-up?' she asked, wrinkling her nose at the dirty pots. 'I'll wash if——'

'No need,' Leith interrupted, 'there's a maid service. Why don't I clear the table, while you shower and get ready for bed?'

'I'd rather do it the other way around,' she told him crisply, 'then if I should happen to leave long hairs you won't find them until tomorrow. By which time I should be feeling more able to cope with your complaints.'

Leith adopted a pained expression. 'Am I that much of a tyrant?'

'Yes!' she declared, and he laughed.

Sian stacked the dishes, wiped the hob and tidied around. She was in the middle of transferring the perishable food from the box to the fridge when suddenly the bathroom door opened and Leith emerged. Wet and dripping, and with a towel slung precariously around his hips, he crossed to her—leaving a trail of damp footprints in his wake.

'No soap,' he announced.

Sian stared. Water beaded the contours of a firmly muscled chest and trickled down his hard, flat stomach. He looked sinewy and strong, a regular he-man. In his clothes Leith gave the impression of being languidly lean, and it came as a surprise to discover he was so well-built. Well-built and disturbingly sexy, she thought. His olive skin gleamed with good health, and the dark, dewy hair on his chest glinted in the light. As if mesmerised, her eyes followed the path of a droplet of water as it ran down his throat, slowly over his chest and torso, to be finally soaked up by the hip-hung towel.

'I was under the shower before I realised,' he said, raking spikes of wet hair back from his brow.

She blinked. 'Sorry?'

'Soap.' He indicated the box she had been unloading. 'I imagine there should be some in there.'

'Oh . . . yes. I'll look.'

Scattering jars and packets every which way, Sian swooped into action until, at last, a tablet was found. She tore off the wrapper and handed it to him.

'I'll call in a couple of minutes and you can come and scrub my back,' Leith told her.

She was to be with him when he was naked? She must touch that glossed, golden skin? Her heart started to thud like a drum. How could he make such a suggestion so casually? she wondered, gazing at him in alarm. Didn't he realise the effect he was having on her? Didn't he know that, while he might treat her with big-brother ease, the emotions which churned inside her were anything but sisterly?

'Scrub your—your back?' she stammered. 'I don't think——'

'Joke, Sian, joke,' he rasped, sounding abruptly irritated.

Rebuking herself for having been so totally out of step, she attempted a recovery. 'I realised that,' she claimed, but Leith had already returned to the bathroom.

Half an hour later Sian was in bed, and yet, although she had stumbled bleary-eyed between the sheets, once she lay down sleep went missing. She tossed and turned. The pillow was repetitively pummelled. She found herself reliving her reaction when Leith had stridden from the shower. Admittedly he was tall and dark-eyed and virile, but he had always been that way. Nothing had changed. So why, after months when her feelings towards him had been serenely *comfortable*, must her knees begin that traitorous wobble? It made no sense. None.

Her lips formed a wry smile. One thing was for certain: as the buzz between them had been one-sided, so was any sexual attraction. Other males might lust after her, but the man sleeping on the other side of the wall did not. If Giles Summerton had found himself in such close proximity, he would have been foaming at the mouth and breaking down the door in wild desire; yet with Leith she was safe. Safe! Sian thought, and felt dramatically and perversely annoyed.

CHAPTER THREE

'TELL me about these politicians you're interviewing,' Sian requested, as she settled herself in the back of the car the following afternoon.

Leith turned to speak to her. 'The first is an elder statesman who's had his finger in the political pie for years, so I intend to concentrate on Chile's past and present with him,' he explained. 'However, the second guy, Carlos Machuca, is the one who really interests me. He's much younger——'

'Thirty-nine,' Raul provided, accelerating away.

'——and my hope is that he'll tell me how he visualises the future.'

'Machuca's a glamour boy. He has long, curly hair and often dresses in black leather. He roars around the city on a big silver motorbike drawing attention to himself,' the interpreter expounded, and glanced in the mirror to seek Sian's reaction.

Obligingly, she grinned. 'He doesn't sound like a British politician!'

'He's a one-off here, too,' Raul acknowledged.

'Yet he's reckoned to be heading for the top,' Leith reflected.

'Some believe so, though personally I feel he's too erratic. Machuca will be championing a cause one minute, but the next he doesn't want to know. It's unusual if he sticks with an idea for more than forty-eight hours. People are increasingly complaining he's unreliable.' The interpreter chuckled. 'His love of the ladies causes some complaints, too.'

Leith's brow furrowed. 'I understood he was married, with five kids?'

'And five mistresses—or more.'

'Whatever happened to reticence?' he muttered.

'You think five mistresses is extravagant?' Sian enquired flippantly. 'You consider Machuca would do better to limit himself to two or three?'

As he swung round, stern brown eyes met hers. 'I consider he'd do better to be faithful to his wife,' Leith rasped.

Although she agreed, his answer took her by surprise. Raul's prurient tone had made it clear that, while he knew he ought not to approve, in fact he took pride in the politician's sexual prowess and envied him his paramours—and she had imagined Leith making a jokey, masculine comment in that vein. Sian frowned. His demand for reliability within marriage seemed an odd counterpoint to his behaviour out of it—and yet she was beginning to realise that her companion was a complex character and a man of paradox.

'I wonder whether Machuca would agree to your snapping him astride his motorbike?' Leith went on.

She peered out of the window. Overnight the breeze had stilled, the humidity had increased, and in place of the cloudless blue hung a polluted canopy of gun-metal grey. Sian sighed. It was the worst sort of light for outdoor photography. 'It's not Machuca who needs to cooperate, it's the brightness,' she told him.

Both politicians occupied offices in the same old-colonial-style government building, but before they could enter stringent checks of identity and purpose of visit were required. After much verification, the soldiers on the pillared portico sanctioned admission, and they were free to cross a lofty hall where cherubs decorated the ceiling and chandeliers glittered. Following instructions, they hiked up stairs, along corridors, beside walls thick with oil-paintings, until finally they reached the minister's suite. A secretary dressed in discreet navy received them and rang through a notice of their arrival. The interview had been arranged for three and, as a clock somewhere struck the hour, double doors were opened and a dignified, silver-haired gentleman appeared. Introductions were made and hands were shaken.

'Encantado de conocerle.' He smiled in a gracious welcome and, after instructing his secretary to take care of Sian, he ushered the two men into his inner sanctum.

She had drunk tea, eaten pastries and taken part in plenty of stilted conversation before the invitation came to join them. Leith's questions had ended and now, the politician smilingly advised, it was her turn. Sian had already decided that his courtliness dictated a mannerly pose, and so she photographed him at his leather-topped desk, beside the onyx fireplace, gazing magisterially out through long windows. Apart from the occasional request for him to move his head—and pleasantries to relax him—she was all concentration.

'You got what you needed?' Leith enquired, as Raul led them back along the marble corridors in search of their second venue.

'Everything,' Sian assured him. 'And you?'

'I was given more than I ever expected,' he reported contentedly.

After what seemed like a mile-long trek, they reached another suite of offices where another navy-clad secretary was informed that Mr Montgomery had arrived to keep his appointment. Again the message was passed on and again double doors were opened, but this time the man who strode out was beetle-browed and surly. He was also, it rapidly transpired, Carlos Machuca's bodyguard.

'He says his boss will not see you,' Raul translated, being apologetic where the body-guard had sounded belligerent and gruff.

Leith frowned. 'Not today?'

'Not at all. The interview has been cancelled.'

'But the guy agreed,' he protested, 'and we have travelled all the way from England.'

'Apparently he's received a death threat,' the interpreter said after a swift exchange, 'and now he isn't willing to meet with strangers.'

Leith swore beneath his breath. 'We may not have met before, but Machuca knows I'm coming. The appointment was confirmed in writing so it's not as though I've turned up out of the blue.' He reached into an inside pocket and drew out his passport and various papers. 'This is a copy of the letter and these are my credentials. Inform boyo here that all his boss needs to do is take a look, and it'll be clear I'm who I say I am and bona fide. The soldiers at the door were satisfied, dammit! Tell him that as well.'

'*No!*' the bodyguard pronounced, brushing aside the translation. A squat, beefy man who was almost as broad as he was tall, he flexed massive shoulders in an ominous gesture.

'Tell him he must show my documents to Machuca,' Leith instructed, remaining unmoved.

'*No!*' the bruiser rejected, before Raul had managed two words.

'I'm not some cuckolded husband come to knife Machuca!' Leith grated. Standing with legs apart, he opened wide the peat-coloured jacket which he wore with a cream polo shirt and dark trousers. 'Get boyo to frisk me, then, when he's satisfied himself I'm not armed, ask if I may speak to his boss for just one minute.'

The request was repeated, but the body-guard stood rigid. Frisking was unacceptable, likewise his employer's granting sixty seconds of his time. Raul appealed, but a refusal was barked out.

'I'm afraid we are, as the phrase goes, banging our heads against a brick wall,' he said regretfully.

'So it seems,' Leith agreed, his voice taut with frustration. 'What I'm not sure about is whether, if we could get past Man Mountain here, it'd do any good. I tend to doubt it. If Machuca's unreliable, it could be he's changed his mind and the death threat is simply an excuse.'

Sian spoke to the interpreter. 'Can't you explain that Mr Montgomery is a highly respected and prominent journalist writing for a highly respected and prominent newspaper, and that an interview will not only ensure the minister's views are read throughout the length and breadth of the UK, but that he'll also be recognised as a leading force in Chilean politics?'

Leith shot her a quick smile. 'Nice try,' he muttered.

An impassioned plea was issued, but, despite Raul's doing everything short of falling sobbing to his knees, at the end of it all the bodyguard remained stubborn-faced and inflexible.

'*Adiós!*' he growled, and stomped back into the inner office and closed the door.

Leith sighed. 'There are good days and bad days,' he said pragmatically.

Behind them, the secretary pressed down a switch and spoke into the intercom.

'This might be one of your good days,' Sian told him.

'How?'

She gave a gleeful grin. 'That was a reminder to Mr Machuca that he has a meeting across town in half an hour.'

'And?'

'We wait until he comes out and grab him.'

Leith shook his head. 'Wise up, Sian. Apart from the fact that Machuca appears to have lost interest in being interviewed—even by my esteemed self,' he inserted drily, 'that wedge beneath Man Mountain's arm was not a packed lunch.'

'He's carrying a gun. I know, I noticed it, too. But if we sneak a word with his lord and master is he going to fill us full of lead? Never,' she declared.

'I agree he might draw the line at bullets, but, *mon brave*, he could still administer a fearsome thump.'

'Or he could call in the guards,' Raul said worriedly, 'and they could lock you up. Lock me up. Lock us all up.'

Leith bestowed a smile of farewell on the secretary and opened the door. 'Let's go,' he said.

'There must be some way of attracting Machuca's attention without causing trouble,' Sian brooded, as they walked down the corridor.

'Forget about it,' he instructed.

'But you wanted that interview.' All of a sudden, her stride halted. 'Wait a minute,' she said.

He threw her a suspicious look. 'For what?'

'*Dónde están los servicios?*' she asked Raul.

Much to her delight, a ladies' toilet was discovered through an archway a few yards on and she dived inside.

'Are you feeling all right?' Leith enquired, when she eventually reappeared some five minutes later.

Sian was wearing a black jumpsuit clinched by a wide green belt, high black boots, and her trilby—and now she tugged at the brim. 'Perfect. Can you hang on while I take a few pictures?' she said, going across to an adjacent window. 'I'd like to get a record of the gardens.'

'They don't look anything special to me.' He frowned as she set down her camera bag. 'Besides, isn't it too gloomy?'

'Not now.'

Step by step, Sian checked the available light, worked out exposures, experimented with first one angle and then another. The few pictures stretched to ten, fifteen, twenty.

'No more,' Leith ordered, when she prepared to install a fresh roll of film.

'But——'

'I thought you reckoned you weren't going to be a nuisance?' he reminded her. 'Sorry, by wasting time like this, you are. There's someone else I need to see and, as we've finished early, this seems like the ideal opportunity. I'll drop you back at the apartment, and——'

'I'm not going with you?' Sian interrupted.

'No need,' he said briskly.

'How long will you be?'

'Hard to say.'

She unscrewed a lens. 'If you don't mind, I'll tag along. I may never come to Santiago again and I'd like to see all I can.'

Leith's jaw hardened. 'As a matter of fact, I do mind. I——'

He broke off as a door back along the corridor suddenly opened and two men strode out. When they turned in their direction one could be instantly recognised as the bodyguard, while the other was a shaggy-headed, sideburned individual in a silver-grey silk suit. Tanned to teak and with gleaming white teeth, Carlos Machuca *was* glamorous—in a swarthy, ageing pop-star kind of way.

Sian gave up silent thanks. At last! Long ago she had read about an actress who prior to an audition had carefully calculated her every move and, in consequence, had walked off with a coveted role; so, now, she replaced her camera, zipped her bag, and waited. Heads down as they talked, the politician and his companion approached—nearer, nearer—until abruptly the bodyguard looked up. Starting in angry recognition, he muttered something which drew Carlos Machuca to a halt. He had stopped several yards away, yet it was close enough. As Leith stood cautiously still and Raul seemed ready to run, Sian stepped forward.

'*Buenas tardes, señor,*' she announced and, with a grand flourish, swept off the emerald-green trilby.

Although her hair had been caught into a pleat when she had left the apartment, in the ladies' toilet it had been unpinned, brushed and, after several experimental runs, painstakingly piled on the top of her head. Now, abruptly released, it tumbled down in slow tassels of silken amber to curl around her face and bounce softly on to her shoulders.

The politician gaped in astonished delight. Gotcha! she thought triumphantly. Then it registered that, beside her, Leith had stiffened.

'Hell's teeth,' he murmured, and she turned to find him gazing at her as if transfixed.

Sian's lips parted in surprise. As Carlos Machuca had been bowled over, so had he. The realisation that she was an adult, attractive and sensual woman had hit. She swallowed down a smile. Leith might not entirely like it—his dark brows had drawn together—but he could no longer deny it. Her image as kid sister was a thing of the past!

'*Buenas tardes, señorita.*'

The greeting needed to be repeated before she realised that the politician was holding out a manicured hand. Sian took it eagerly.

'Er——' in the heat of the moment, her Spanish failed her '—we came to keep an appointment, but——'

'There appears to have been a breakdown in communications,' Carlos Machuca apologised, smoothly switching to English. 'You wanted to see me, but for some reason this fellow——' the bodyguard received a ferocious glower '—decided to keep us apart.' He squeezed her fingers. 'A grave error.'

Leith stepped forward to make introductions. 'So I'd like to interview you,' he completed, frowning at their still clasped hands, 'and Miss Howarth is here to take your photograph.'

The politician's eyes wandered over the lines of her body as he mentally, but blatantly, stripped her naked. 'I'd prefer to take yours,' he told her, with practised confidentiality. 'You're far more interesting.'

'I understand you have a meeting right now,' Leith went on, in clipped tones, 'so maybe tomorrow——'

'The meeting can wait, but an English Rose?' Her admirer paused and leaned closer. 'Never,' he purred.

Sian withdrew her hand. 'Thank you,' she smiled.

As they headed back to the office, Leith gave her a ghost of a wink.

Over the next three hours, Carlos Machuca demonstrated that, although his addiction to the opposite sex was strong, two other drugs provided an instant kick—his own voice and his own appearance. When Leith finished the interview, the politician yattered on, pronouncing about this subject, dissecting that, telling interminable anecdotes about his past which, without exception, managed to demonstrate what a fascinating, witty, *dazzling* individual he was. And when strained vocal cords indicated even to him that he had said enough, he became enthralled with the business of having his picture taken. Carlos Machuca gazed into mirrors and spent ages combing his hair. Others had insisted his left profile was his best, did Sian agree? he asked, parading like a peacock. How about a shot of him with his jacket removed, maybe his shirt unbuttoned, or suppose he stretched out on the chaise-longue? And, finally, would she make certain he received ample copies of all the photographs she had taken? There were those, he confided, who would adore one.

It was dark by the time they prised themselves free. Raul dropped them back at the apartment then hurried home, and not much later they re-emerged and headed for a seafood restaurant which was conveniently situated on the next block. The food was good and the meal relaxed, but when they returned Leith immediately set up his portable computer.

'There are some extra notes I want to make and if I don't do them now I'll lose them,' he told her.

'Are we to have a dirge as background inspiration?' Sian enquired sassily.

Whenever they travelled both of them took along personal stereos, though Leith's came equipped with additional side-speakers which he used in his hotel room when he worked. There was a second divergence—her taste ran to popular music, while he preferred classical.

'Not if you're going to sit here with your fingers jammed in your ears,' he replied.

'I won't.'

He arched a brow. 'You mean at last you're learning to appreciate decent music?'

'I mean I'm off to have a bath!'

Aware that he would write better if he was left undisturbed, Sian took her time. Her hair piled on top of her head, she enjoyed a long soak before washing and leisurely drying herself. A fragrant talc was dusted over her skin and she pulled on a pair of pale jade satin pyjamas.

'Finished?' she asked, coming out to find the music still playing and Leith sprawled in an armchair.

'For now. I'd like to thank you for your help with Machuca.' He frowned down the length of his legs. 'You made quite an impact.'

Sian grinned. 'Machuca made an impact on me, too.'

'He did?' Leith grimaced. 'I thought tight jackets and winkle-picker shoes went out with the sixties.'

'Maybe, but the wrap-around dentistry was spectacular.'

'Ditto his aftershave. The fumes were so strong you could lean on them.' He nodded towards the bathroom. 'All clear?'

'All yours,' she confirmed, and he disappeared.

The music he had chosen was a selection of pieces conducted by the Austrian maestro, Herbert von Karajan. Left alone to listen, Sian was forced to admit that the increasing tempo of Ravel's drums did hold a certain fascination, but ... She removed his tape and inserted one of her own.

'Hey!' Leith poked his head out of the bathroom door. Still dressed, he was in the middle of cleaning his teeth and the brush which was stuck in his mouth did not encourage conversation. 'You ... can't ... do ... that,' he gargled.

'I've done it,' she replied.

'But it's ... sacrilege to cut off a ... monumental piece like ... the "Bolero" just when it's ... reaching the climax. Put it back on.'

'After you've finished your teeth and had your shower.'

'Now.' He shone a foamy smile. 'Indulge me.'

'Go jump in a lake!' Sian said irreverently.

'But ... this stuff ... is pure ...'

'You don't need to devote yet another forty-five minutes to detailing the limitations of Luther Vandross, Chris de Burgh, Billy Joel and Co,' she cut in. 'I received that lecture in Washington.'

Leith vanished. In the bathroom there were sounds of running water and him finishing his teeth, and then he came out again.

'Let's listen to the final build-up,' he appealed, walking over and picking up his tape.

'When you've had your shower!'

'Two minutes, that's all.'

'Don't you dare,' Sian threatened, as he positioned an olive-skinned finger above the switch.

'He who dares wins,' Leith recited.

His finger dive-bombed; the music cut out; she leapt up.

'You don't win this time,' Sian declared and, snatching the Karajan tape from him, she dashed into her bedroom and slammed the door.

Feverishly, she looked around. Where could she hide it? In a drawer? Under the bed? There was no chance to decide, for a moment later Leith burst in.

'Give that to me,' he ordered.

She giggled. 'No way. You've lost it now.' From the corner of her eye she caught sight of the open window. 'Hah!'

Sian was halfway across the room when he pounced, grabbing hold of her by the waist and wrestling her down on to the bed. She laughed, twisted herself around and pushed hard against his shoulders, but he tightened his grip, his fingers sliding on the slippery satin of her pyjamas.

'This is unfair use of brute strength,' she protested.

'So complain to the ombudsman.'

'I'm complaining to the brute in question,' Sian retorted, and thumped a fist against his chest.

In the struggle which followed her hair fell loose and a couple of buttons unhooked themselves on her jacket.

'Oh, no, you don't!' Leith panted, as she held the tape out at arm's length and aimed to fling it.

She gave a deep-throated chuckle. 'Oh, yes, I do.'

'Struth, you're bloody-minded,' he accused.

'Tell me something I don't know,' Sian gasped.

In an attempt to capture her flailing arm he climbed astride her, a knee on either side of her hips and—abruptly—all wrestling ceased. She looked up at him. He gazed down at her. His entrapment was so close, so intimate, so inherently sexual, that it changed everything. A circuit connected, a current flowed, and for a long, electric moment their eyes clung. A pulse beat at Leith's temple. Exposed in the V of her half-open jacket, Sian's high breasts rose and fell.

'I will tell you something you don't know,' he said hoarsely. 'Sian, I have a wicked crush on you.'

Her heart stopped, and started again. Adrenalin surged. She felt dizzy with pleasure, saturated by excitement. Vaguely she was aware that Leith's blink rate had increased, which indicated he must be as nervous as she.

'You're—you're going to give me a forty-five-minute lecture on that?' she faltered, when he continued to gaze down at her.

'Sticking to a lecture would be the wisest thing, but——'

'But what?' Sian asked, waiting, hoping.

He wanted her, she had seen the charged, naked emotion in his eyes. And she wanted him. She wanted his arms around her. She wanted his mouth on hers. She wanted——

'I knew all along this was bound to happen,' Leith said, in a tortured voice.

'All along?' Sian protested. 'Surely it was only this afternoon, when I did the trick with my hair, that——'

He shook his head. 'For months now, keeping my distance has been imposing a terrible strain on my natural impulses.'

'It has?' she said wonderingly.

'You never realised I was keeping things relentlessly platonic while all the time I've been crazy about you?' Leith gave an impatient sigh. 'I thought I could orchestrate and control, but

I was deceiving myself. You just need to come near, Sian, and I can't breathe properly!'

She uncurled her fingers and, unheeded, the tape slid on to the quilted cover. All of a sudden, she knew he had not been alone in his self-deception. Somehow, when and where she was least expecting it, she had been caught, and now she was forced to acknowledge that she, too, cared. The buzz had not been derived from working in unison, but simply from being *with* him—and when he was around everyone else tended to smudge into the background. Why hadn't she been aware of this? Sian wondered. Because Leith had been determinedly nailing down the lid on his feelings and, in consequence, hers. Sexual attraction had been rejected, ignored, denied. But now she understood why she had rushed so eagerly to his home. Why she had fought so violently against being excluded from this trip. Why, when he had revealed that *he* had excluded her, it had felt like the end of the world.

'This is why you didn't want me here, isn't it?' she said. 'You were frightened you'd no longer be able to control things?'

An emotion she could not define flickered across his eyes, then Leith replied, 'Yes.'

'Now I understand your tension. At the time I didn't think it was my fault, but——'

'What tension?' he demanded.

'Come on,' Sian protested, 'the nearer we got to Chile the jumpier you became, until when we landed it was as though someone had used a spanner and tightened your nerves to breaking-point.' She grinned. 'I assume the prospect of our sharing an apartment was troubling you?'

'Yes,' he said again.

She reached up, and with her index finger outlined the curve of his full mouth and its indented corners. 'And "it" shouldn't happen?' she enquired softly.

He shook his head. 'No.'

'Why not?'

'Because—oh, hell,' he moaned, and he leant forward and his body was hard on hers and he began kissing her, his tongue searching the quivering depths of her mouth. 'Sian, I need to make love to you,' he muttered.

'And I want you to.'

Leith pulled back. 'Even so, I'd rather we didn't,' he began to say, but his protest faded as she unloosened the remaining buttons on her jacket and the pale satin slid away. 'You don't believe in making things easy,' he complained, gazing at her creamy-skinned breasts, with their delicate tracing of veins and taut honeyed nipples.

'On the contrary.' Sian smiled, and slithered out of her trousers.

He made a sound of dissent, but then, as though unable to help himself, he trailed his long fingers over the swelling curve of one breast and down across her stomach to gently touch the tangle of red-gold curls between her thighs.

'You have the body of a siren,' he sighed, and his mouth covered hers.

Sian's skin tingled; her breasts tightened; she felt a searching ache. Urgently, her hands went to his shirt buttons and on to the buckle of his belt.

'You're built like a lumberjack,' she told him, when he was naked.

'Gee whizz!' Leith exclaimed, in droll amusement.

She drew her fingers over the muscles of his shoulders and chest. 'It's a compliment. A lumberjack who tastes of toothpaste,' she said, when he kissed her again.

His kisses continued, their fervour increasing, and he began to stroke her, his fingers fondling her breasts, grazing her nipples, exploring the secret places of her thighs in long, lingering caresses until every cell of Sian's body seemed to be inflamed.

'Sweetheart,' he sighed, and bending his dark head he lapped his tongue around the sensitive, straining peaks of her breasts so that she gasped, arching beneath him.

With an incoherent murmur, he slid into her. Heat flooded through her body, and Sian cried out. An explosion was coming, growing, gathering, building. Her body contracted in rhythm, forcing a moan of ecstasy from him.

'Sian,' he muttered, in a low, harsh voice. 'Oh, Sian, oh, sweetheart, oh, darling, oh, *yes* . . .'

'We'd better get some sleep,' Leith said, much later. 'I don't know about you, but if I don't have at least ten minutes a night I'm cranky the whole of the next day.'

'So sleep.' Sian smiled.

'How can I with you lying beside me with your hair spread across the pillow, and that silky skin, and those luscious breasts?' He groaned. 'We've made love twice already. I'm not supposed to be in a state of high arousal again.'

'You're aroused?' she enquired, with mock innocence.

The hand which cupped her hip moved her closer. 'You'd better believe it.'

'I do.'

'I want to kiss you until our mouths are ablaze, and wrap myself up in your hair, and pour champagne into your every orifice, and——'

'There's no rush,' Sian murmured. 'You'll get round to everything in time.'

Leith's expression stilled. 'You reckon?'

'I reckon, though I wouldn't refuse a kiss or two now,' she said, nestling even closer.

They made love again.

CHAPTER FOUR

WHEN Sian awoke the next morning, she awoke alone. Fondly she touched the empty pillow beside her and then stretched, luxuriating in the deliciously satisfied feel of her body and her happiness. This was *it*, she thought. This was the feeling which illuminated people, made them glow, made their mouths never want to stop smiling—and now it had happened to *her*! She sighed, remembering how completely she and Leith had fused together. There was only one word to describe the chemistry which existed between them: sublime. Yet they had more on their side than sexual affinity. Those months when they had worked together, talked together, laughed together, had been wonderfully worthwhile, in that they ensured their relationship was built on the firm foundation of *liking*. Sian's happiness rocketed into a flying sense of elation. Today was the perfect day for running barefoot through fields of daisies!

More mundanely, she located her pyjamas and, pulling them on, padded barefoot into the living-room where Leith was sitting at the table eating breakfast. Dressed and newly shaved, he had brewed coffee and prepared some toast.

'Hello, ratface.' She grinned.

'Good morning.'

She had been about to hook her arms around his neck and kiss him, but a formality in his greeting stopped her. Studying him closer, she saw that his expression was tight and his brown eyes sombre.

Sian pushed tangles of flame hair from her eyes. 'Are you feeling tired?' she asked.

'No—surprisingly.' The watch strapped to his wrist received a frown. 'You'd better hurry up and get showered. Raul will be here in three-quarters of an hour.'

Washing and dressing were speedily accomplished, then she fixed her hair into a gleaming twist at the nape of her neck, made up her eyes, dashed on lip-gloss and, fifteen minutes later, joined him. Sitting down, she helped herself to coffee.

'We must sleep apart,' Leith announced suddenly.

Sian quelled an internal flutter of disappointment. Earlier he had claimed not to be tired, yet in the interim he had apparently decided it would be wise to catch up on some rest. Had jet-lag prodded a finger?

'For tonight.' She smiled. 'Fine.'

'No, for the rest of our stay.'

She had been reaching for the marmalade, but her hand stopped in mid-air. 'For the rest f our stay?' she echoed, unable to take the equired leap of the imagination.

He nodded. 'Do you want to move into a otel or shall I?'

This must be some bizarre joke, Sian de-ided, struggling to think with a brain which uddenly seemed to be packed with cotton wool. Any moment now, he would grin and tell er he was kidding.

'Oh, Leith,' she protested, beginning to augh, 'I——'

'One of us must, it's the only way. Last night we rushed into bed on impulse and without hinking things through. It was sheer animal attraction,' he declared, so fluidly that she re-lised the argument had been rehearsed. His mouth produced an engaging grin. 'But I'm sure you agree with me that conducting a per-sonal relationship within a work situation is fraught with problems and better avoided.'

With shaky fingers, Sian groped for the jar. He did not intend their love-affair to continue, to mature, to ripen? An abyss opened up in her heart. But he *must*!

She took a breath, priming herself to speak. 'As a matter of fact, I don't agree,' she said.

'But if it became known that something was going on between us it would destroy the balance in our dealings with everyone else at the *Vulcan*,' Leith protested, his frown indi-cating that this dissension was both unexpected and unwelcome. 'Attitudes would alter and become strained.' He paused, and for a moment seemed bogged down. 'Plus, people in high places could disapprove of an involvement and mark it against us, and our careers would suffer. I know how important your career is to you,' he finished, in triumph.

Sian sat rigid. The feelings of unhinged disbelief and despair which had swamped her seconds ago had shifted into an anger which burned deep and fierce—anger at him, but also anger at herself for her naïve behaviour. She had known of Leith Montgomery's reputation. She had been aware of the risks. She had been warned she became involved with him at her peril—and yet she had taken no notice. Why? Because when his eyes—dark and soft and steady—had looked into hers, she had felt she was with the most sincere man on earth. Because she had, she supposed, subconsciously believed herself capable of bucking the trend. Sian, the reformer? Sian, the love of his life? She gave a bitter inner laugh. What a joke! Plastering a slice of toast with marmalade, she raised it to her mouth, but promptly put it down. Her appetite had disappeared.

'Self-justifying twaddle!' she proclaimed. 'You're simply making up excuses for what you want to do.'

Leith blinked. 'I beg your pardon?'

'For a start, we're not together all day and every day under constant surveillance so it would be simple to keep any relationship a secret. But even if the news did leak out, I can't see why it would be disastrous,' Sian said, trying to sound curtly reasonable rather than defensive and emotional, though it was not easy. 'There are couples at the *Vulcan* who are either dating, living together or who are married, and none of their careers have taken a tumble.'

'Perhaps,' he agreed, with reluctance, 'but——'

'I haven't finished. However, I know all this is immaterial and that whatever I say will change nothing because——' her eyes flashed green fire '——I know you have decided to give me what is commonly termed the Old Heave-Ho, the Spanish Fiddler, the Bullet.'

Leith recoiled from her choice of words. 'Sweetheart,' he appealed, 'I——'

'Don't sweetheart me!' she snapped. 'It's bang, finished, all over. Yes?'

He looked at her for a long, still moment. 'Has to be,' he said, his voice expressionless.

Sian glowered. When something was over, it was over, and she supposed there was something to be said for knowing where she stood. She might not like it, but at least she knew.

'Oh, for a convenient bread-knife,' she said grimly.

'You want to murder me?' he enquired.

'In a manner which would cause prolonged and extreme agony.'

Leith's mouth took on a wry slant. 'You wouldn't settle for grabbing hold of my lapels and flinging me against the wall?'

'This might seem laughable to you, but it isn't to me,' she retorted. 'You give the phrase "a brief affair" a whole new meaning. I realise now I was gullible, but I never imagined you off-loaded your women quite so quickly!'

He frowned. 'I didn't want to sleep with you and I never intended to. It was an accident,' he defended.

'An accident?' Sian gave a caustic laugh. 'Great! Knowing I was merely one of life's kerbstones over which you happened to trip makes me feel a whole bunch better.'

'Believe me, if we continued to—to be lovers we would both get hurt,' he said in a low voice.

'Both? You mean you'd suffer? My heart bleeds.'

Leith lifted a teaspoon, and began turning it over and over. 'Don't let's make this heavy,' he appealed, and shone a smile of entreaty. 'Last night was really no big deal.'

'You mean you were playing a game of Trivial Pursuit?' she demanded.

He looked beyond her. 'Yes.'

Sian's stomach churned. What had happened was not a new story, it happened every day, but how could she have been so rash—and so deceived? Get hurt? She *was* hurt—woefully. And as for his dismissing last night as insignificant...

'I don't deny that impulse drew us together, but while physical gratification began and ended it for you, in making love, dumbo here——' she jerked a thumb at her chest '—was also demonstrating that she cared.'

His tongue moistened his lips. 'You're very up-front, aren't you?'

'You mean none of your other rejects have ever looked you in the eye and complained?' Sian queried. She might have made things easy last night, but she refused to make anything easy for him now. 'I suppose you'd prefer it if I shrugged my shoulders, muttered something about it being nice while it lasted, and filed the experience away under lessons learned? Well, sorry, but for me, and for most women if they're honest, going to bed with someone is a darn sight more complicated than that!'

'I'd prefer it if you accepted that calling a halt is the best way,' Leith said heavily.

'You're doing this for my own good?' Sian derided. 'You're telling me this is an event I should celebrate?'

He released a sigh. 'I am.'

As Leith looked at her across the table, she noticed his eyes flicker to the curves of her breasts beneath the white silk blouse. Their impassioned rise and fall appeared to fascinate him. Sian stiffened. That he might find her anger sensual was a development she had neither anticipated, nor wanted.

'How very philanthropic!' she barked, fighting the urge to clamp her arms across her chest. 'Well, there's no need to worry about *me* becoming a habit. And as for long goodbyes—whatever happened to them?'

He forsook the teaspoon. 'Couldn't you once, just once, function in the rational rather than the reactive mode?' he enquired. 'If you think about things you'll see that——'

'You know the ideal woman for you?' Sian cut in. 'Someone who makes love like a fiend until dawn and then turns into a toasted sandwich!'

Leith pushed his fingers through the thick dark hair which curled around his ears. 'Let's be civilised about this,' he appealed.

'I am being!' she rasped.

A stagnant pool of silence formed.

'How many lovers have you had?' he asked, after a while.

'Two, including you,' Sian replied stonily.

'A novice,' he muttered. 'Who was the first one?'

'A guy I met at college. He was my boyfriend for four years.'

Leith raised his eyes to the ceiling. 'Oh, hell.'

'Don't worry,' she said curtly, 'I may not be the most experienced of females, but this is the end of the twentieth century so I'm not about to yell rape!'

His mouth thinned. 'Just as well, because it wasn't. You were as keen as I to make love. If not keener. I made my reluctance plain, but, if you remember, you unfastened your pyjama jacket and——'

His eyes fell to her breasts again, and to her fury she felt her nipples begin to tighten.

'OK, it takes two to tango,' Sian said quickly, unwilling to be reminded of just how wanton and uninhibited she had been, 'but the difference between us was that I had no idea I was participating in a one-night stand, and had I done I wouldn't have.' Her chin lifted. Although her distaste at being picked up and so precipitately dropped down had been rammed home, it was vital she draw the distinction between herself as an angrily wronged woman and some snivelling, broken-hearted female. 'However, as you once said, I'm a tough butterfly and by this time tomorrow I'll have recovered,' she declared. 'One night of misplaced passion doesn't enrol *me* in the ranks of your walking wounded!'

'You make it sound as though I've turned romance into some kind of blood sport,' Leith protested.

'Haven't you? Tell me, how many victims have you clocked up this far? Ten? Twenty? More?'

At the jibe, his dark eyes began to smoulder and his nostrils flared, making him look very Latin, very proud, very dangerous. 'Contrary to what you appear to believe, ninety-nine per cent of the time the only thing which accompanies me to bed is an improving book!' he grated, slamming his hand down on the table in emphasis and making her, and the coffee-cups, jump. 'And, while I don't profess to wear a halo, I have always been honest in any relationship.'

'Which, translated, means if some besotted female gets hurt it's her tough luck?' Sian taunted.

Leith's teeth ground together. 'It means that the women I've dated have always known exactly what they were getting into.'

'And what they would be chucked out of?' she asked, in a baiting voice. '*I* didn't know.'

'You're the exception,' he said tersely.

'And our relationship is the exception, too— in that it's the one you're not being honest about?'

Leith scowled. 'Explain.'

'We both know your talk of trouble at the office is rubbish, so why not come clean and confess the real reason for giving me the elbow,' Sian demanded. She forced herself to take a mouthful of coffee, and voice the question which had begun scratching away at her mind.

'Maybe you found my performance last night a little...lacking?' she suggested.

'No.' He rubbed savagely at his brow. 'Sian, you lack nothing. Nothing,' he insisted.

Amid her pain and anger, she felt a tiny spurt of satisfaction. So the chemistry she had imagined *had* existed and had been as overwhelming for him, too. Puzzled, she looked across the table. 'Well...?'

Leith hesitated, clearly unsure what to say. 'I——' he started, at last, but the intercom buzzed. 'That will be Raul. We'll need to finish this conversation later,' he said, his relief transparent and immense.

Sian shook her head. 'I need to finish it *now*. Is it a woman?'

'A woman?' He walked over to speak into the plastic box fixed beside the door. 'Raul? Hi. We'll be down in a couple of minutes.'

'Are you involved with someone else?' she demanded, as he came back to collect his jacket and briefcase. 'Is that why——?'

'You're right.' He smiled, and lifted a broad shoulder.

The breath sucked through her throat. That smile and oh, so casual shrug symbolised the ruthless way he had trampled over her emotions, his careless dismissal, his *treachery*.

'You cheat on her, make me an accessory, and it doesn't matter?' Sian demanded, flinging back her chair. Hands spread on her hips, she

glared. 'You talk about animal attraction—
you're the only animal here. You're a jackal!
A toad! A twenty-four-carat shark!'

'A shark happens to be a fish. However, reluctant as I am to stop you in full invective, I
still need to know which of us is going to move
into a hotel,' Leith said tightly.

'Me,' Sian announced, deciding she had no
wish to sleep again in that so recently and
rapturously shared bed.

'OK. Adriana's lined up a number of businessmen, so the game plan for today is to interview one this morning and a second in the
afternoon. However, there's a gap around
lunchtime which should give us enough time to
book you a room, come back here and transfer
your stuff.'

'You book the room. I won't be joining you
this morning,' Sian told him.

Leith flung her an exasperated look. 'I'm
sorry about what's happened, but there's no
need to be——'

'I might even contact the airline and book a
flight home,' she declared.

'Come on, that's silly,' he protested.

She frowned down at her feet. 'I won't leave,'
she muttered, 'but I am staying in.' When she
raised her head, her mouth was tight and her
eyes were defiant. 'I'm damned if I'm going to
dance to your tune. Maybe where work's con-

cerned you are the boss, but in every other area you're a——'

'Save the speech,' he instructed, and slung his jacket over his shoulder. 'We'll see you around one. You'll need to lock me out,' he told her, striding towards the door.

As she watched him step on to the landing, Sian's fingers curled into fists. Half an hour ago—thanks to him—she had been floating in a world of dreams come true and happy endings, but now—thanks to him—it had been shattered into a thousand aching pieces.

'I hate you,' she declared impetuously.

Unflinching brown eyes met hers. 'I know,' Leith said.

Although it was obvious that Leith regarded her refusal to join him as juvenile—and telling him she hated him probably had been—Sian was acting out of an instinct for self-preservation. Anger had been gluing her together but, without warning, the adhesive had lost its grip and she had been on the brink of falling apart. Once she had worked everything out she would reconcile herself to the reality and things would not seem so bad, she told herself, but working things through would be impossible with the perpetrator of her unhappiness close at hand. She needed time alone, a breathing-space, and then she would bounce back.

For the next hour or so, Sian mooched around the apartment, thinking, thinking. She felt lost and confused. How could she have been so wrong about a relationship which her intuition had insisted was gloriously right? she wondered. How could she have been so easily duped? To be fair, Leith had protested his unwillingness to make love, until she had coaxed him on. But he had not protested *that* much, she thought, her eyes sparking with resentment, and she refused to accept responsibility for his sins.

Halfway through the morning the maid, a plump, fortyish woman in a maroon overall, arrived. On discovering Sian could speak some Spanish she started to chat—and chat—only to realise she was running behind schedule. Wary of getting in the way of someone who had become a cleaning dervish, and because a change of scene seemed like a good idea, Sian went for a walk. After yesterday's grey, the sky had capriciously returned to blue, and the sun shone mellow and golden. Half a mile along the road, and beyond the cinema Raul had mentioned, she found the shopping mall. A supermarket and multitude of smaller shops filled the ground floor, while the upper floor housed a modern and luxurious department store. Sian wandered inside and spent time looking around the fashions. The sweaters, shoes and leather goods were particularly attractive.

When she returned, the apartment was neat and tidy, and the maid had gone. Sian packed her suitcase and stood it ready with her camera bag, beside the door. One o'clock arrived, but Leith did not. At two, when she was still on her own, she made herself a sandwich. Could he have telephoned during her absence and, via Raul, left a message with the maid? Interviewing required a fluid schedule and sometimes demanded an impromptu change of plans. Yet, although she looked, there was no message to be found.

At three o'clock it occurred to her that, as she had refused to play ball in the morning, so Leith might be paying her back by being deliberately uncooperative this afternoon. Was he staying out of touch in order to teach her a lesson? Sian wondered. For all his faults, it did not seem the kind of trick he would pull, and yet . . .

Leith would be back by five at the latest, she told herself as the afternoon lengthened, but the deadline ticked by uninterrupted. Attempts were made to read a paperback which had absorbed her on the plane, but it had lost all interest. As she ate another sandwich and drank several cups of coffee, six and seven o'clock came. Sian grew increasingly restless. Leith must return soon, or at least phone. But perhaps he and Raul were stuck in a traffic jam somewhere? Or the car had broken down? Maybe one of the businessmen had launched into a diatribe and, Carlos-Machuca-style, could not be stopped? There was no need to fret, she told herself. If anyone could fend for themselves, it was Leith Montgomery! Yet—maybe it was due to being in a strange country, or because she hadn't a clue where he had gone, or perhaps she was still on edge from the morning's disturbance—her anxiety spiralled. Why hadn't he come back? What could have happened? Had some disaster befallen him?

When the intercom buzzed at seven-fifteen, Sian flew to answer it.

'Hello? Leith?' she demanded, forgetting all about her intention to be offhand and cool.

'This is Raul.' The Chilean cleared his throat. 'I regret to advise you that Mr Montgomery has been involved in an accident. I'm here to take you to the hospital.'

Sian gaped at the intercom. There *was* a disaster! Her certainty that Chile held no dangers had been absolute, but now pictures of Leith being mugged, beaten up, or even shot, clicked one after another through her head like gruesome slides through a projector.

'What—what kind of an accident?' she faltered.

'I understand he was knocked down in the street, by a truck.'

A piercing pain left her breathless. 'But—but you weren't with him when it happened?' she asked, in bewilderment.

'No. Please come down and I'll explain on the way.'

Flinging her striped jacket over her shirt and grey trousers, Sian grabbed her bag and hurried down to the car. Raul barely waited until she was installed in the passenger seat beside him before he set off.

'How badly injured is he?' she demanded, as they sped down the road.

'I don't know. The hospital said it isn't their practice to give details over the telephone and all they would tell me was that he had broken some bones and was in shock. However, if it was a truck which hit him . . .' The interpreter made a small, expressive gesture, and said no more. He did not need to.

Sian's insides clenched. 'How come you weren't together?' she asked again.

'I start at the beginning,' Raul said pedantically. 'After Mr Montgomery had finished this morning's interview we attempted to reserve a hotel room, but as there is a dental conference plus a mining seminar taking place in town it was difficult. Only when we reached the Sheraton did we find a vacancy.' He cast her a glance. 'Mr Montgomery explained how your stay at the apartment last night was due to some confusion at your newspaper in London.'

'That's right,' Sian agreed, too wound up in the current calamity to speculate on what Raul might have thought of the arrangement or what reason Leith had given for her absence today.

'Unfortunately there was a drawback in that the room wouldn't be available for several hours,' the interpreter continued, 'and so Mr Montgomery rang to explain and, because you were out, I spoke to the maid.'

'I didn't receive any message.'

'No? The woman said she'd tell the porter and he could tell you.'

Sian frowned. 'The porter wasn't at his desk when I came through the lobby and it never occurred to me to check whether he'd heard anything.'

'And he didn't ring up to you?' Raul's click of an admonishing tongue was followed by an intrinsically Latin shrug of acceptance. 'Mr Montgomery wanted to let you know that his next interview had been brought forward, and so he'd be busy at one o'clock and onwards,' he explained. 'He said as you couldn't move into the hotel to please remain at the apartment, and he'd pick you up in a taxi late afternoon when the room would be free.'

'You weren't coming for me in the car?' she queried.

'No. Today is my wife's birthday and as we were celebrating with a party at home Mr Montgomery agreed I could finish early.' Raul slowed for traffic-lights, and when the green sign shone pressed his foot down on the pedal again. 'We'd just sat down to eat when the hospital phoned,' he said ruefully.

'How did they know to phone you?'

'Fortunately he was carrying my business card. The second interview took less time than expected,' the interpreter said, continuing his recital, 'and afterwards Mr Montgomery told me there was someone else he wanted to speak to. I offered to take him, but he said they spoke English and he would use a taxi and my services were not required.' He spread a hand. 'So I went home.'

Sian frowned, recalling how yesterday when the Carlos Machuca interview had seemed unlikely Leith had been all set to disappear and, presumably, visit the same person.

'Did he say who it was he wanted to see?' she asked.

'No. I had the impression it could be personal.'

'And it was during his visit to them that he was knocked down?'

'I imagine so. The hospital representative said the truck failed to stop,' Raul went on, 'and there was some confusion and delay before an ambulance was summoned. However, Mr Montgomery has been taken to one of Santiago's leading medical complexes.' A minute or two later, he peered ahead and indicated a white tower block with turquoise-tinted windows. 'We are here.'

As she climbed from the car, Sian took a steadying breath. No matter how fraught their relationship, there could be no place now for hostility. She was Leith's sole companion and link with home, and he was totally dependent on her. It did not matter that her experience of hospitals was minimal, nor that her knowledge of foreign medical rituals rated zero; it was her duty to make sure he received the best possible treatment and to provide whatever support—practical and emotional—he needed.

Her stomach knotting tighter and tighter, Sian went with Raul into a spacious, modern-art-adorned lobby. Here people waited in hushed clusters and white-coated medics strode through. She did her best to understand the conversation between the interpreter and the receptionist, but they spoke so quickly that after a sentence or two she was lost.

'At present Mr Montgomery is in a room off the main accident ward,' Raul explained, shepherding her around a corner and along a corridor, 'but he's due to be moved. His wounds have been cleaned and treated, and they've done everything possible for the time being. The doctor in charge is attending to another emergency, but as soon as he's available he'll see us in his office and explain the situation.'

A turn to the right and right again, and a sign announced that they had arrived at their destination. Raul commandeered a passing nurse, and after a few rattled-off words she directed them to a side room.

'She said Mr Montgomery has concussion and is confused and sleepy, but he has not been sedated.' The Chilean bent in a polite bow. 'Please, *señorita*, after you.'

Sian walked forward, steeled herself, and opened the door. With floor and walls tiled in stark white, the room was small and strictly functional. A faint smell of disinfectant hung in the air. In the centre, below the single bright light, stood a trolley-type stretcher. She stepped up to it. Leith's eyes were closed and his breathing shallow; tousled dark hair was matted damply across his brow. A sheet came up to his waist and he was bare-chested. In dismay, her gaze travelled over him. His left side, it was painfully apparent, had taken the brunt of the collision, for his left cheek was torn and swollen, and grazes trailed in bloody patches down his jaw and on to his throat. When they reached his shoulder, the grazes spread into a wide swathe of cuts, abrasions and bruises which marched across his chest and down. The broken flesh had been smeared with ointment and an intravenous drip fed saline into his arm. Sian swallowed down the lump which had formed in her throat. Leith looked haggard, vulnerable and amazingly young.

Tentatively, she touched the olive-skinned hand which lay on the coverlet. There was no response, but at least it felt warm. For a minute or two Raul stood with her, frowning over Leith and offering whispered commiserations on his injuries, then he gave a shamefaced smile.

'Would you mind if I leave you for a few minutes?' he asked. 'Hospitals always make me jumpy and now I would like to smoke a cigarette.'

'Go ahead,' she said.

When the interpreter had gone, her eyes refastened themselves on the man in the bed. The last time she had seen him he had been fit, alert and unblemished, but now... Sian swallowed again.

'Why did you have to get yourself smashed up?' she scolded softly. 'What happened, did you forget that the traffic drives on the opposite side of the road here? That was foolish.'

'Not foolish,' Leith mumbled, and his eyes opened—dark brown eyes which were unseeing and glazed with pain. 'Bloody stupid!' he exclaimed, and his hands began to clench and unclench, his fingers clawing at the white cotton sheet. 'Should have known. Should have guessed. Should have gone sooner.' Anguish contorted his face. 'I left it too late.'

Sian flinched, alarmed by the vehemence of his anger. 'Hey,' she protested, 'anyone can make a mistake crossing the road.'

There was a long pause. 'I want my mother,' he muttered, his throat working convulsively. 'I want her but she's gone.'

Her heart turned over. Leith might be thirty-four years old, yet he sounded like the plaintive and stricken child he must have been all those years ago when his mother had walked out.

'If she'd been there,' he mumbled. 'But she wasn't there. It should never have happened. The bastard shouldn't have done it. Cruel. Didn't give a damn. Didn't give a damn about me,' he said, the words emerging jerky and broken. 'Knew I was hurt and bleeding. Didn't care. Didn't help. Just cared about himself. His life. His future.'

Possessed by a sudden urge to touch him, to somehow *help*, Sian reached out and brushed the dark hair from his brow. 'Shh,' she soothed. 'I know the driver didn't stop, but you're safe now.'

Although the assurance sounded inadequate to her ears, it seemed to comfort him, for the clawing fingers stilled and he fell silent. A minute or two passed when Leith seemed to be sleeping, then his eyes opened again.

'Sian?' he asked, and she saw that his gaze had steadied into a sharper focus.

'Hi.'

He gave a faint smile. 'You got your wish. I am in extreme agony.'

Her stomach hollowed. 'When I said that I didn't mean it.'

'You did, but,' he added, with a laboured breath, 'I would have done better to have taken on you and a bread-knife than a ten-ton truck.'

'The fight does appear to have been rather uneven,' Sian agreed ruefully.

'Most I could have done was dent the grille, but I've had chunks torn out of me and cracked my ribs.' When Leith hunted for breath again, she saw that the few short sentences they had exchanged had drained him. 'You were right about Conchali,' he muttered.

'Conchali?' she asked, but once more his thoughts had begun to meander.

'Only thing you were wrong about is me and I was wrong about everything. Every single thing,' he said, and his voice held a note of despair. 'All my life I've believed that—what does it matter?' he said, gazing at her with tormented eyes. 'It doesn't. Nothing matters.' His lids closed. 'Nothing.'

'Is Mr Montgomery asleep?' Raul asked, when he opened the door a short while later.

Sian nodded. 'He did wake up, but not for long.'

'The nurse says the doctor's free and could we go and see him.'

The doctor, a short, bespectacled, fresh-faced young man, was waiting behind his desk. After requesting that they be seated, he introduced himself as Bernardo Mardones and launched into swift Spanish which, when Raul explained that Mr Montgomery's *amiga* came from the UK and he would need to translate, was promptly altered to a swift American-accented English. The doctor had, he informed them, done part of his medical training in the United States.

In between fielding telephone calls and dealing with numerous in-and-out visits from nurses, Doctor Mardones told her that, although Mr Montgomery's superficial wounds would quickly heal, a series of tests needed to be done. These would take a day or two to organise, but the delay was no bad thing because her friend had suffered a major trauma and it would allow him time to rest.

'What kind of tests?' Sian enquired.

'Bone scans, computerised tomography—that means X-rays which are taken using a computer.'

'These are to check the state of his ribs? Leith told me he'd cracked them,' she said.

'They're on his spine. What are called myelograms will also be scheduled. That involves a liquid being poured down the spinal column in order to——'

'Sorry, but I don't understand your interest,' Sian interrupted. 'I must be missing something.'

Doctor Mardones frowned. 'Your friend did not tell you about his . . . disability?'

'What disability?'

'He is unable to move his legs.'

Sian's heart seemed to shrink, as if protecting itself from what she was being told. 'Then his spine was—was damaged in the accident?' she faltered.

'It looks like it. Our tests will reveal the extent and whether or not his condition is permanent, but——' the young man gave a sorrowful smile '—I'm afraid that Mr Montgomery is paralysed from the waist down.'

CHAPTER FIVE

THE moment Sian returned to the apartment she hunted down a pen and paper, and determinedly started to make a list. In times of stress her tendency was, it had to be admitted, to respond emotionally and in a somewhat slapdash fashion, but the present situation demanded a more mature approach. Organisation was the key. Already several matters which needed her attention had surfaced and, given the chance to think, she would doubtless identify more. Though the time difference meant she could not contact London until the morning, of paramount importance was passing on the news of Leith's accident to Giles Summerton. At the hub of the call must be finance for, after dropping his bombshell, Doctor Mardones had—with apologies—moved on to basics. Who, he wanted to know, would be picking up the tab for Mr Montgomery's medical expenses? Whatever the length of his stay, they would not come cheap. Sian had explained that, like all the newspaper's employees, when he travelled Leith carried insurance, but that, in any case, the journalist enjoyed the backing of a large and prosperous publishing group.

The doctor was sorry; verbal assurances were not enough. The hospital's rules demanded a written guarantee of payment—soonest.

The phone call placed on 'hold', one immediate task was to discover whether Leith had brought pyjamas and, if so, put them ready to take to the hospital tomorrow. Reluctantly, Sian went into his bedroom. She did not relish looking through his belongings—it seemed both presumptuous and too *intimate*—but she made a thorough search—and came out empty-handed. It was no surprise, for, although she could not decide why, Leith had seemed the kind of male who would invariably sleep naked. Sian frowned, biting deep into her lip. He had slept naked with her the previous night. Smooth-skinned naked. Firm-limbed naked. Magnificently and carelessly naked...

Picking up her pen, Sian wrote 'buy pyjamas' on her list. She must also remember to take along his toothbrush and other toiletry items. What had happened to the clothes he had been wearing at the time of the accident was something she would need to discover, plus the whereabouts of his wallet and briefcase. Were any of the articles he had written waiting to be transferred to London? If so, action was required there. The list lengthened. She must find out from Leith whether there were more interviews arranged, and, if so, cancel them. Anything else? Sian was on the verge of deciding all contingencies had been covered when the Sheraton booking was remembered. By now it had gone eleven; did she have the energy and inclination to make a move? No. Could she sleep again in the once-shared bed? Yes, if necessary. She called the hotel to cancel the room, only to discover it had been re-let when she had not shown.

Wearily, Sian made a cup of coffee and carried it from the kitchen to the sofa. The distance was no more than four or five strides, yet as she sat down it struck her—like a blade in her back—that those few strides were more than Leith might ever walk again. The cup in her hand began to shake, the coffee swilling over the rim so violently that she was forced to put it down. 'No,' she whimpered. 'No, no, no!' She drew up her knees and, wrapping her arms around them, lowered her head. Hiccupping tears, she began to cry. It was a long time before she stopped.

The following morning Sian rang the *Vulcan* and, ignoring twinges of distaste, asked to speak to Giles Summerton. She waited, and when the editor's secretary advised that he was away attending a conference, gave a sigh of relief and had herself transferred to Alan Barnes' extension instead. Explaining what had happened and what needed to be done took time, but eventually they had the financial side arranged.

'And it will be a few days before Leith receives the final verdict?' the photography chief recapped.

'Four or five,' she confirmed.

'So all the poor fellow can do is wait, and wonder whether he'll ever again stand upright.'

Throughout the call Sian had been purposefully matter-of-fact, but now her throat became constricted and when she attempted to speak nothing emerged.

'I'll fill Giles in and everyone else here,' Alan went on, oblivious to her distress, 'but what about Leith's family and friends? Is there anyone who should be informed?'

She gulped in a breath. 'I suppose his stepmother, Dorothy, and——' Sian hesitated '—his girlfriend.'

'What's her name?'

'Don't know. Let's leave any notifications until later,' she said briskly. 'According to the doctor Leith should have recovered from his concussion and be making sense today, so when I see him I'll ask who he'd like to be contacted—and ring you.'

'Ring in daily,' came the instruction. 'I guess all we can do at present is take things one day at a time.' Alan sighed. 'Leith must be wondering why he ever insisted on going to Chile—and cursing himself.'

'*He* insisted?' Sian questioned. 'Giles Summerton didn't send him?'

'Nope. Leith's assignments are usually arrived at via a joint decision, but this one was his brainwave. Giles didn't reckon much to it—said nothing of any importance was taking place in Chile at the moment—but Leith pushed like hell.'

She frowned. 'I wonder why.'

'No idea. Don't quote me,' Alan continued chattily, 'but the only reason Giles agreed was because he was scared that if he upset his *numero uno* he might decide to cast a more favourable eye on the opposition's overtures.'

'They're trying to poach Leith?'

'Have been for ages—though if the guy *is* doomed to spending the rest of his life in a wheelchair their interest will dry up overnight. Mind you, being in a chair wouldn't stop him from writing. What it would mean is——'

'This call must be costing a fortune,' Sian cut in, unable to take any more. 'I'll be in touch tomorrow.'

When the line had been cleared, she rang the hospital and, in careful Spanish, asked for an update on Señor Montgomery. His condition was described as 'comfortable' and he had been moved to a private room on the third floor, the receptionist reported. Doctor Mardones wished the patient to have an undisturbed morning, but visitors would be welcome in the afternoon. Sian passed the information to Raul and they agreed on a time for him to take her, then she went out and purchased a pair of pale lemon pyjamas.

In contrast to the spartan accident ward of the previous night, Leith's room was luxurious. The slub-linen walls and thick carpet were of a muted oyster, while apple-green printed curtains hung at the windows and an apple-green quilt covered the bed. Raul was particularly impressed. After the initial greetings, he launched into an enthusiastic appreciation of the décor, which only ended when he abruptly felt the craving for a smoke. Best wishes to Mr Montgomery. He would wait in the car. Goodbye.

'All this will need to be paid for,' Leith observed, when they were alone. 'If you get in touch with London they'll——'

'I have and everything's been arranged,' Sian said.

His brows rose. 'Yes?'

'I might be gauche in some areas, but I'm not entirely incapable,' she told him pertly. 'My intelligence does occasionally rise above dingbat level.'

A nerve beat in his temple. 'So what's the score?' he demanded.

She detailed her phone call to Alan, and then took out the pyjamas. 'Do you think they're big enough?' she asked.

He checked the tag. 'Just my size. What did you do, grab hold of the nearest lumberjack and tell the assistant you wanted something to fit him?' Leith enquired drily.

As had been predicted, although his grazes looked, if possible, even more horrific than yesterday and he was covered in a Technicolor riot of purple and yellow bruises, mentally Leith was back to normal. Almost, for although he was alert he seemed preoccupied with his own thoughts. A state of affairs which, Sian acknowledged, was to be expected.

'You guessed,' she said, then, reluctant to dwell on what had prompted her lumberjack remark, continued quickly, 'As these are OK, I'll buy you another pair.'

'Better make it two. I'm oozing blood from wounds all over the place.'

Sian's stomach cramped. 'You're still in agony?'

'No. I just feel as though someone's worked me over with a cosh, but I guess that's par for the course if you jaywalk,' Leith dismissed.

'What colour of pyjamas would you like?' she asked weakly.

'Don't mind. Could you also bring in an English-language newspaper?' he requested. 'A boy comes round with papers here and I tried to ask if he could get me one, but I couldn't make him understand.'

'Will do. I'll also have a word with the nurse and see if she can arrange for you to receive an English paper on a daily basis.'

'Thanks.' Leith cast her a glance. 'And thanks for visiting.'

Sian sat straighter in her chair. 'You think I'd abandon you?' she demanded.

'No.' He paused. 'Another thing I'd like to know is whether or not there's a choice of food. They gave me liver for lunch, and——' he pulled a face '—yuck!'

'I'll make enquiries,' she promised, 'and maybe it would help if I bought you a Spanish-English dictionary?'

'Please.'

Sian took out her notepad. 'Alan was asking who should be informed of your accident. If you give me the names and phone numbers I'll pass them on to him.'

'No one's to be contacted,' Leith replied.

She looked at him in surprise. 'You're sure?'

'I'm sure. Dot's away for a month and it wouldn't be fair to spoil her holiday, and I don't see the point in alarming anyone else.'

'Shouldn't your girlfriend be told?' Sian asked, becoming busy checking down her list.

'Who? Oh. No.' Painfully, he shifted his position on the pillow. 'Let's get the tests over first. The doctor explained what's going to be done, and why?' he demanded.

She nodded. 'At first I didn't know what he was talking about because I didn't realise you'd damaged your spine.' She darted him a look. 'When I was here yesterday you told me about your ribs, but you never mentioned that.'

'I must have forgotten.'

'Forgotten?' she repeated, in wide-eyed disbelief.

'I was woozy.'

'Maybe, but you did talk about——'

'I'm aware of the hole I'm in,' Leith interjected, 'but the sun will still rise and set even though I'm a paraplegic.'

Paraplegic? Sian flinched. The concept was so new and so devastating, it amazed her he could even say the word, let alone use it so carelessly.

'You—you may not be,' she gulped.

'Wishful thinking. Look,' he said, when she began to protest, 'in hard-rock terms the prognosis is not good. The doctor reckons my spine may have been either crushed or broken somewhere in the region of the second or third lumbar vertebrae—and I'll bet ten to one it's broken.'

'He quoted at least a fifty-fifty chance to me,' she objected. 'He also said you have strong bones. He said that, although your ribs are cracked, the damage is far less than he would have expected and that outwardly your spine doesn't appear to be in too bad a shape at all.' Sian eyed him quizzically. 'Didn't he tell you?'

'Yes, but when I walked out into the road the truck I walked in front of was *big*.'

'You make it sound as though you strolled into the traffic regardless,' she protested, wondering how he could be so indifferent—to his accident, to the resultant wounds, to the possible consequences.

'I did. I told you I jaywalked.' Leith frowned. 'I had . . . thoughts on my mind.'

She waited for him to tell her what the 'thoughts' had been, but he didn't. Instead he sat there, pensive and withdrawn, as though he were on another planet. Sian frowned. She could not explain it—you would need to be a trained decoder to read the man—but she was beginning to have the feeling that there could be something going on inside him which took precedence over his immediate predicament. Yet what could be more compelling than the possibility of being paralysed?

'It was lucky your wallet and briefcase were handed into the ambulance,' she remarked.

Leith nodded. 'Very. Please would you take them back to the apartment, together with my jacket and other things?' he said, indicating a neatly folded pile of clothes on the locker. 'The jacket's torn and may not be worth keeping, but perhaps you could check?'

'No problem,' Sian replied, and was thrust back into thoughts of *his* problems and his reaction to them.

Leith might be permanently disabled. He appeared to believe he would be. But where was the gnashing of teeth, the railling at fate, the *angst*? In his place, she would have had a single thought rolling endlessly and horrendously around in her head—would she ever walk again? Yet now he was asking if she would tell the nursing staff he preferred his windows left open! Sian sighed. His attitude was confusing.

'Is there anything else you'd like tomorrow?' she asked. 'Tissues, fruit——'

'A bottle of mineral water, please. And could you find out from the nurse whether there's any routine to the doctor's visits? I saw him for ten minutes this morning, but since then——' The door opened and Doctor Mardones walked in. 'Don't bother,' Leith said, 'I can ask him myself.'

The young man greeted the two of them and, as he checked the chart which was clipped to the end of the bed, smiled across at his patient.

'I thought you'd like to know that those first tests we discussed have been fixed for tomorrow.'

Leith nodded. 'Fine.'

Doctor Mardones came to check his pulse. 'Had any sign of feeling in the legs yet?'

'None.'

Wary that an examination might be imminent, Sian got to her feet. 'I'd better be on my way. Raul's been waiting for ages.' She gathered up the clothes and Leith's briefcase. 'I hope all goes well with the tests,' she said, with an encouraging smile. 'Bye.'

She called in to see the sister in charge of the floor and, after passing on Leith's requests, made her way to the lift lobby. Sian had pressed the call button when the march of footsteps sounded, and Doctor Mardones joined her.

'Your friend's a cool customer,' he remarked, as they waited. 'So self-possessed. So self-contained. When people are faced with the possibility of an "acquired" disability their first reaction is usually a strenuous denial. This *cannot* be allowed to happen. It *isn't* possible. But he hasn't denied anything.'

Sian frowned. 'Leith does seem amazingly stoical,' she agreed.

'He isn't even clutching at the perfectly legitimate hope that his paralysis may be temporary. Most patients would be hitting me with question after question in a desperate bid for reassurance, yet he's raised no queries.' The young man cast her a glance. 'Perhaps this is an example of the famous English stiff upper lip?'

'Could be,' she said doubtfully, 'though Leith's only half-English.'

'The other fifty per cent is Chilean? I thought he bore more than a passing resemblance to a local.'

'The other half is Spanish,' Sian said.

'Almost the same thing.' Doctor Mardones shrugged. 'The bulk of our population is descended from the Castilian and Andalusian conquerors.'

A bell pinged and the lift arrived.

'You don't think Leith's cool is a bit...strange?' she enquired, as they went inside.

'It's unusual,' the doctor concurred, 'but shock can have a curious effect. Maybe he's dealing with the situation by not dealing with it?'

'Maybe,' Sian agreed, though she was not convinced.

The next few days were an uneasy mix of hospital visiting, telephone reports to the *Vulcan*—and to her parents—and long hours when there was nothing to do but pace the floor, worrying and wondering. Yet Leith did not appear to worry and wonder—at least, not about his condition. On the contrary, he remained resolutely detached, incurious, and still distracted.

'How are you feeling?' Sian asked, the morning after the myelograms.

'Much better. My ribs are improving. All it needs now is to get these healed,' he said, gingerly touching the grazes on his jaw, 'use the razor, and I'll be almost human again.'

Wryly she eyed the blue-black growth which had transformed his clean-cut looks into those of an unkempt, yet dashing, ruffian. All the nursing staff, she had noticed, positively *pandered* to him.

'Half-inch stubble is the ''in'' thing,' she said.

'Half-inch stubble itches like hell!' Leith retorted. A sister came in to take his temperature. 'Could you ask her when I can have a shave? I worked out what I thought was the correct phrase and asked twice when she was in earlier, but all I received were smiles and blank looks.'

As the thermometer was inserted into his mouth, enquiries were made and an answer of 'in a few days' was given. Sian waited until the woman had disappeared, and then perched herself on the edge of the bed.

'After the tests did—er—the technicians give any kind of indication?' she asked haltingly.

'As to the state of my backbone? No. The results are being passed to the good doctor, who needs time to assess them.'

'He's had time,' a voice said, and Doctor Mardones walked in holding a sheaf of negatives. 'You stay,' he told Sian, when she hesitated, wondering whether this was her cue to hightail it out of the room.

Her stomach twisted. If the doctor wanted her around it followed that the news must be bad—didn't it? Sian had promised herself that when the moment of truth arrived she would be composed, take it calmly and, if necessary, offer the ultimate in support, but her body suddenly started to act in a way it was not supposed to. The strength drained from her limbs. She felt weak and light-headed. To her dismay, she discovered her hands were trembling. Sian clasped them tightly in her lap and, when she had summoned up a measure of control, consciously loosened them. She took a breath. She was ready—as far as she ever could be.

Leafing through the X-rays, Doctor Mardones held one up to the light. 'Mr Montgomery, this shows your spine has not been fractured and that the crushing is so slight as to be virtually no more than a bruising.'

Sian's heart leapt. 'So he'll walk again?' she demanded.

The young man grinned. 'The neurologist and I can see no reason why not.'

A huge wave of relief crashed over, knocking her composure to smithereens and making her hands tremble again. 'Isn't that wonderful?' she jabbered, and lunged forward to grab hold of Leith. 'I was so...and you were...oh, thank goodness.'

'Careful of my ribs,' he warned.

Abruptly aware that not only was she in danger of hurting him, but she was also in danger of making a fool of herself, Sian jerked back. Pleasure at the news was one thing. Hauling her one-time, one-*night* lover into a clinch was another. 'I'm delighted,' she muttered, pink-faced and prim.

'May I take a look?' Leith requested, and the doctor passed him the X-ray. 'I don't understand why, if my spine's only been bruised, my legs are still deprived of movement,' he said, studying it.

'I don't understand that either,' Doctor Mardones confessed. 'Initially the shock of the impact appears to have paralysed, but now...' He shook his head. 'However, I'm sure it will be only a day or two before full sensation and mobility return.'

His patient put the negative aside. 'Why are you sure?' he asked.

'Because other functions which are governed by the same nerve-bundle have returned to normal—the control of your bladder, et cetera.'

'And if everything else works, my legs will?'

The younger man nodded confidently. 'That's the way it goes.'

Brimming with hope and expectation, Sian went into the hospital the next day, but Leith's condition remained static. It was most disappointing. Tomorrow would see an improvement, she assured herself—and him—but to her dismay the improvement did not happen. You must be patient, Sian insisted in a private lecture, yet when nothing changed the day after that, either, it was impossible to prevent her disappointment tumbling through bewilderment into alarm. The physiotherapist who had been brought in to massage and exercise Leith's legs pronounced on their excellent muscle tone, the X-rays were checked and re-checked, other tests were done, yet he continued to be paralysed. Why? On the fourth morning, a nurse intercepted Sian on her arrival and said that Doctor Mardones would like to speak to her.

'I thought I ought to warn you that your friend is not in a good mood,' the young man smiled ruefully, 'and explain. You see, as we can find no medical cause for his disability, the obvious next step is to consider whether the problem might be psychological.'

'You think he isn't walking because subconsciously he doesn't want to?' Sian said, in surprise.

'There will be all manner of complexities involved, but basically—yes.' He pushed his glasses further up his nose. 'However, when I raised the possibility with Mr Montgomery he was not receptive, and when I suggested counselling he started to shout.'

She grimaced. 'Oh, dear.'

'I wondered whether you could have a word and try to persuade him to at least consider what I said,' Doctor Mardones continued. 'You know him far better than I do and maybe you can succeed where I failed. You could also tell him that by the end of the week he'll be fit enough to make the journey home. I did intend to inform him myself—until he lost his temper.'

'But Leith's losing his temper has to be healthier than his previous apathy,' Sian said.

'Healthier for him maybe,' the young man agreed, with a boyish grin, 'but anyone entering his territory goes in fear of their lives.'

She laughed and, with a promise to try and help, made her way to the third floor.

'Is it safe to come in or are you going to hurl abuse and pill bottles?' Sian enquired, peering around the door to find Leith sitting up in bed.

'You know,' he said flatly.

She walked across to place the magazines she had brought on to the locker beside him. 'Yes, Doctor Mardones revealed all.'

'Have you ever heard such a load of——' he frowned, searching for a more acceptable word '—horse manure?' was what he came up with. 'You'd think I was some featherbrained housewife who has nothing better to do with her time than take a fit of the vapours!'

'Sexist,' Sian said.

'OK, you'd think I was featherbrained. Full stop.' Leith raked an exasperated hand through his hair. 'My paralysis may be all in the mind? In other words, I'm reckoned to be suffering from some form of deep-seated hysteria! Struth, I'm a clear-headed, profoundly sensible adult——'

'One who's had a shave,' she cut in.

'Don't change the subject,' he grated. 'And yet Mardones has the nerve to tell me I'm *imagining* I can't walk! What's he playing at? Does he think I'm lying in this bed for fun?'

'It isn't a matter of intelligence or imagination,' Sian began, but got no further.

'The guy's labelled me a fraud!'

She shook her head. 'What he has done is recognise an avenue to be explored and in my opinion he——'

'I might have guessed it—you subscribe to Mardones's theory!' Leith accused, and pointed a finger. '*You're* in league with him. The kid must be fresh out of college and yet *you*——'

'Just because he's young it doesn't mean he doesn't know what he's talking about.'

He gave her a drop-dead look. 'Doctors have made faulty diagnoses before.'

'True,' Sian said, removing her jacket and laying it over a chair. 'But I still consider he may have a point of view.'

'And I have two useless bloody legs!'

'You've also seen the X-rays.'

'To hell with them! And to hell with Mardones!'

She perched on the edge of the bed. 'Aren't you the one who advocates being rational rather than reactive?' she queried, with a sweetly arch smile.

'I'm the one who knows when his own limbs can't—not *won't*—work!' Leith slammed back, his brown eyes blazing. 'No one in their right mind would ever *choose* to be paralysed!'

'But the point is that you aren't choosing—not consciously. What the doctor seems to think is——'

'Don't forget there's a sexual side to this,' he muttered.

Warily, Sian looked at him. 'Sexual?'

'Think about what we shared the other night. Do you honestly believe I'd never want to experience anything like that again?'

Her pulse tripped. She sat very still. She did not appreciate his reminder of the hours she had been trying so determinedly to forget, nor did she care for the way he was using them to illustrate the wish that his future would include making the same ecstatic love to other women.

'I suppose not,' she said shortly.

'But if I'm disabled that side of my life will be limited. Then maybe the best I'll ever manage is——' Leith reached out and, grabbing hold of her shoulders, drew her roughly forward '—this!'

His mouth ground down, hard on hers, and his tongue penetrated her lips. Caught by surprise and off balance, Sian fell against him. It took a moment for her to summon up the wit to protest, but the harsh possession of his mouth stifled any words at source and when she tried to pull away his grip tightened, his fingers biting into her flesh. Even as an invalid, Leith was far stronger than she. Trapped against the muscled wall of his chest, Sian's blood began to race. Her skin prickled. Her heart hammered wildly against her breastbone. She had never experienced such a violent demonstration of raw emotion. With this angry and abrasive kiss, Leith was making her stingingly aware of his physical needs—and, regrettably, her own.

When he released her, he glared at her, his chest rising and falling. 'Understand?' he bit out.

Aware that he had been simply clarifying a point—if intensely—Sian gazed steadfastly back. 'I do,' she replied, her voice level. Feeling rather like a swan which looked serene on top while paddling desperately away beneath, she rose and walked to the window. 'Doctor Mardones asked me to pass on the news that you'll be well enough to travel home at the weekend,' Sian said, gazing blindly out at the streets below. 'I'll contact the airline and make enquiries about how it can be arranged.'

'I'm not ready to leave yet.'

She spun round. 'I beg your pardon?'

'I want to stay in Chile. If I'm stuck in a bed, I might as well be in Santiago as anywhere. No need to break into a cold sweat,' Leith went on brusquely, 'you can go home. I know you're keen to get back there.'

'Am I?'

'You threatened to go last week,' he reminded her.

'Oh ... yes,' Sian acknowledged, trying to decide why he did not want to depart. Maybe the rigours of making such a long journey as an invalid frightened him? Maybe he didn't relish the prospect of being seen on a stretcher and in a wheelchair in public? Maybe he simply felt more secure staying put? 'But London's one of the world's foremost medical centres and if you go home you'll be able to see a top-flight specialist and get a second opinion on your legs,' she protested.

'I don't need a second opinion. Whatever Mardones or any other doctor may think, I know the problem is entirely *physical*. They're my limbs, dammit! Very soon Raul's time with us expires and then there will be no one to ferry you to and from the hospital,' he announced, swerving on to a different track.

'I can use the underground,' she told him. 'I've already made enquiries and the journey's straightforward.'

Leith scowled, annoyed to find her one step ahead. 'I still think it's better if you go,' he persisted. 'You're due out on Monday, but there's no need to wait until then. Why not bring your flight forward?'

Sian lowered her head, chains of flame hair spilling forward to half hide her face. Not content with banning her from his bed, was he now intent on shuffling her out of the country at the speed of light? Being advised she was so utterly dispensable did wonders for the ego!

'But if I leave there will be no one to visit you,' she replied, in a matter-of-fact voice. A gesture was made towards the items on the locker. 'There will be no one to fetch and carry. No one to talk to.'

'I can talk to the doctor, and to Raul,' he declared, his face hardening into mask-like rigidity, 'and I'm making headway with my Spanish.'

'You might manage a phrase or two, but it falls far short of communication,' Sian argued. 'And your contact with Doctor Mardones and Raul will be perfunctory at best.'

'You'll be telling me next I can't live without you,' Leith growled, and his fingers balled into fists. 'I repeat, there's no need for you to stick around and watch the freak show.'

Sian winced. 'Leith——'

'I don't need a woman close at hand!'

'Don't you mean *under* your hand?' she shot back, but the flash of irritation was short-lived. Losing her temper would not help, no matter how exasperating and hurtful he might be. She was the one able to stand on her own two feet and so she was the one who must make allowances and show forbearance. 'If I walked away and left you lying in a hospital bed in a foreign country I'd never be able to live with myself, never be able to sleep nights,' she informed him. 'Leave? No way, José.'

'But I don't want anyone in attendance, dammit! I never wanted you here in the first place—remember?'

Sian shivered, chilled by the coldness in his eyes and in his voice. She did remember. She also remembered how good everything had been between them—could have been—until he had ripped it to pieces. As Alan had said, Leith Montgomery was a marauding panther, prowling through the jungle of life leaving a trail of carcasses behind him. But, right now, he was a *wounded* panther.

'I shall stay—for a while anyway,' she said. 'I was speaking to Giles Summerton yesterday and, like Alan, he insists you're the first priority and that my work takes second place. There's absolutely no pressure on me to return.'

'And what will you do during the time you're not at the hospital?' he demanded.

'I can look up Jill's parents, and meet Raul's family—he's been asking if I'd like to see his kids—and take photographs, and——'

Leith expelled a breath. 'Sounds as if you have a hundred and one reasons for remaining!'

'There's a reason for everything,' Sian replied, then paused, frowning over the cliché. She walked slowly towards the bed. 'For instance, there's a reason why your past is littered with failed relationships.'

He tensed. 'Sian,' he threatened.

She refused to be deflected. In trying to uproot her, he had punched straight from the shoulder, so why shouldn't she have her say?

'You profess to be clear-headed and profoundly sensible, so you must have sussed out why it is whenever you become involved with a woman you invariably let her down.'

His face took on a strained and remote look. 'I don't wish to continue this conversation along its present lines,' Leith said curtly.

Sian retrieved her argument without comment. 'The relationship with the mother is said to be at the root of all relationships, and in your case it could be you're both craving her and then seeking to avenge yourself for her walking out.'

'That's very inventive!'

'I'm explaining reasons,' she said quietly.

'The hell you are!' Leith snarled. 'All you're doing is propounding cock-eyed and impertinent opinions about my private life—and you have opinions the way Hindu gods have arms. Quit hectoring me, Sian!'

'It's wrong to ignore what happened in your childhood,' she carried on. 'You must accept that the suppression of emotional pain leaves scars and——'

He silenced her with a savage, slashing gesture of his hand. 'Jargon! Thanks for the psychiatric investigation; I suppose now, Doctor Freud, you're going to explain why my legs are refusing to work?' he enquired bitterly.

Sian sighed. 'No.'

'Your homespun philosophy doesn't stretch to a reason for that?' Leith jeered.

'Unfortunately not.' She was silent for a moment, then she picked up her jacket and walked to the door. 'If you tell Doctor Mardones you're staying, I'll let Giles Summerton know you'll be here for a while longer.' Sian straightened her shoulders. 'And that so will I.'

CHAPTER SIX

FOR the next two weeks Sian continually begged the gods to make Leith mobile again—he must, please, tomorrow?—and continually her prayers went unanswered. His scars and bruises faded, his ribs began to mend, but the paralysis remained. A second time the doctor suggested counselling and a second time his patient dismissed the idea outright, and so, where it mattered, the fortnight frustratingly ended at the same point at which it had begun.

'We appear to have reached stalemate,' Doctor Mardones told Sian, meeting her one morning as she made her way along the third-floor corridor. 'In fact, I've decided to discharge him.'

She shot a bewildered glance sideways. 'Isn't that a bit drastic?' she protested. 'Doesn't Leith still require nursing care?'

'Some, though he can obtain that elsewhere. The point is that being ejected might be the stimulus which will get him walking again.'

'You reckon he needs a stimulus?'

As they reached Leith's room, the young man stopped. 'I reckon he needs some kind of a shock which will break through the mental barrier he appears to have erected and, with luck, this could be it.' Opening the door, he strode in. 'Good morning,' he said breezily, 'any change with the legs?'

'You mean since yesterday when you propped me up between bars and I sweated gallons trying to move one inch, but didn't?' Leith asked sardonically. 'No.'

'Then it's time you left. I'd like you on a plane and into a hospital in England as soon as it can be arranged.'

Surprise flickered across the screen of Leith's eyes, but was swiftly deleted. 'I suppose bouncing me out is your idea?' he accused, frowning at Sian.

She shook her head. 'Not guilty.'

'It's mine,' the doctor told him. 'We don't appear to be able to do anything more for you, so——'

'I'll leave, but I'm going back to the apartment,' Leith declared, throwing a challenging look in Sian's direction.

She did not react. Although her daily visits were amicable, there had been an undercurrent of strain. Leith continued to wallow in introspection, and since her analysis of the whys and wherefores of his love life had also been aloof. Not so aloof that anyone else would notice—indeed, when she had brought along Jill's parents they had remarked on how agreeable he had been—but enough to dampen their usual camaraderie. The conversation which had once been so easy between them was in danger of tailing off into a superficial non-speak. Being a fleeting conquest, and an outspoken one at that, was, it had become apparent, quite the worst qualification for being a friend.

'Your choice, so long as the accommodation's available,' she said. 'I'll check.'

'You'll need a wheelchair and various other disablement aids,' Doctor Mardones warned, 'plus the services of a physiotherapist and a part-time nurse to help you bathe.' Leith shrugged agreement. 'Then—then I'll fix everything with Miss Howarth,' the doctor said uncertainly.

'Please do. I'd like to be gone by tomorrow.'

Later, when a phone call to the apart-hotel had extended their booking, the practicalities had been organised, and an early afternoon departure time arranged, the doctor admitted to Sian that his plan of provoking Leith into action appeared to have backfired. Neither panic, excitement nor fear, all or any of which he had hoped to incite, had materialised. Instead dismissal had been calmly accepted, with the patient proceeding to dictate his own terms!

'All we can do now is keep our fingers crossed,' the young man remarked wryly, as they said goodbye.

By the time she returned to the apartment it was lunchtime, so Sian assembled cold chicken,

lettuce and coleslaw and made herself a salad.
Settling for crossed fingers seemed woefully in-
sufficient, she thought, as she ate. There must
be something *constructive* someone could do.
But what, and who was that someone? The
physiotherapist and nurse would attend to his
daily welfare, but as from tomorrow the only
person with an ongoing interest in Leith's plight
would be her. A sigh escaped. Two weeks ago,
his taunt about her being unable to provide an
explanation for his continued paralysis had
spiked itself in her mind, and she began to consider it again. Wary as she was of being accused of yet more amateur psychology, it
seemed to her that Leith's mental barrier—if
one existed—could have been triggered by
something which had happened on the night of
the accident. Sian's brows drew together. In the
aftermath his haphazard conversation had
centred on lacerating himself and the truck
driver with recriminations, though he had, she
suddenly remembered, also mentioned
Conchali. Why Conchali? It seemed an odd
reference . . . unless that was where he had been
knocked down. So did the person he had been
visiting live there? But *whom* had he been
visiting and could they have any bearing on his
emotional state? Raul had reckoned his call to
be personal, yet this was Leith's first time in
Chile so whom could he know? She sighed. He

had not named names, and it seemed doubtful now that if she asked him he would tell her.

Snap! Like a jigsaw-puzzle shape, a piece of information slotted into her mind. He knew Adriana Sanchez, a woman he had described as 'very pretty'. Sian put down her knife and fork. She had automatically assumed his girl-friend would come from England, but... Could Adriana be the other woman? Was she the reason why Leith had 'pushed like hell' to come here, and—her thoughts streaked on—why he had not wanted her to accompany him, and why he had been reluctant to make love? Had Adriana been on his mind when he had jay-walked under the truck? Was she why he had been so distracted ever since?

Sian's face began to burn. When Leith had declared he did not need a woman close at hand, he had been specifically referring to *her*—but maybe the motives she had attributed to his not wishing to leave Chile were so much rubbish? Had he insisted on staying because he wanted to be with Adriana? Was the intention for his fellow journalist to move into the apartment and shower him with plenty of tender, loving care? There had been no mention of them communicating, nor of Adriana visiting Leith in hospital, but she had not been with him twenty-four hours a day and he could have asked Doctor Mardones to be discreet. Sian squirmed. All the time she had been insisting he needed her help, had Leith been attempting to oust her in favour of the Chilean woman?

The telephone rang, shrilling through her thoughts, and she went to answer it. Her caller was Raul who, despite having moved on to another interpreting assignment, had kept in touch and provided a comforting presence.

'What's the latest with Mr Montgomery?' he enquired.

She brought him up to date, and then said as nonchalantly as she could, 'I understand Adriana Sanchez acted as go-between with you and Leith?'

'Ah, Adriana,' the interpreter sighed. 'She has a bungalow at Viña del Mar, and if you saw her on the beach there you'd never believe she was fifty-two years old and a grandmother. Such a delicious creature. Mmm.' He made a kissing sound. 'But her husband is jealous. He'd murder any man who made the slightest approach. Did you have a query about her?'

'No, no,' Sian replied, 'I was just confirming the name.'

'Must go, but next time I ring perhaps we can arrange for you to come out to my house again?' Raul suggested.

'That would be nice,' she agreed, thinking of the two happy evenings she had already spent with his family. 'Bye.'

Farewell to Raul. Farewell to Adriana. Back to square one. Who lived in Conchali? she wondered, resuming her lunch. As she drank her coffee, Sian's thoughts began to surreptitiously steal towards Leith's briefcase and the address book he kept there. Uneasily, she chewed at her lip. All her instincts rebelled against snooping and she knew he would be furious, but if she was to assist ... With many misgivings, she located the book and began flicking through. When she reached page 'L', she stopped. A 'Maria Leiva' resided in Conchali. The name rang no bells. Who was she? After being so thoroughly adrift with Adriana Sanchez, Sian felt disinclined to make guesses. Instead, having checked there were no other Conchali addresses, she slipped the book into her shoulder-bag, collected her camera equipment, and went down in the lift. The porter summoned a taxi.

Thirty minutes later, it had become clear that the district which Leith had initially claimed to be wealthy but had later acknowledged as poor was *very* poor. A conglomeration of corrugated-iron-roofed shacks, cement blocks of low-income flats and clay houses which, she supposed, were *haciendas de adobe*, Conchali lay to the north of the city, hidden behind the San Cristóbal hill like a blemish better not seen. When the taxi-driver stopped, Sian climbed out into a land of the poverty-stricken and

neglected. Focusing her camera, she began to
snap toddlers clambering over a wrecked and
rusty car, a pack of scavenging dogs,
schoolboys playing *'fútbol'* on a patch of
wasteland.

Her photographic appetite temporarily sated,
she started off along the pot-holed street
looking for the written-down address but in-
termittent numbering of the houses made
identification difficult. Sian stopped and re-
newed her film. It did not matter. This opportunity to take pictures was highly satisfactory,
but where her original purpose was concerned
the journey had been a dead loss. Maria Leiva,
the surroundings made it clear, was someone
from the lower reaches of Chilean society
whom Leith must have arranged to interview.
His visit had not been personal and therefore
lacked any emotional significance.

Sian was frowning at the address book, and
toying with the idea of searching out the
woman's home and taking photographs to accompany any article which Leith might eventually decide to write, when one of the footballing
schoolboys appeared alongside. Squinting over
her arm, he also read Leith's scrawl.

'Maria Leiva?' Energetically, he shook his
head. 'Filomena Leiva—*si*!' he announced, and
clutching at her arm the boy began propelling
her towards a shabby wooden cottage.

'*No*,' Sian protested. She put the address book into her bag and took a firmer grip on her camera. '*Muchas gracias*—um—*usted hacer un error*—no—um—I mean——'

'*Inglésa?*' the boy asked.

'*Si*,' she agreed, hurriedly trying to assemble the right words to tell him he was making a mistake and that she had no wish to make contact with the presumably absent Maria nor to disturb Filomena—whoever she was.

'Hey, *Señora Leiva*!' the boy yelled. '*Inglésa.*'

To her embarrassment, at his shout the door of the cottage opened and a tiny, silver-haired old lady came out. She wore a neat, though well-mended, black dress, and as she walked forward her carriage was stately and erect.

'I am one of the few people here who know English,' she told Sian, in an accented voice, 'so anyone speaking the language tends to be brought to me.'

Showing no displeasure at having been so summarily summoned to meet a stranger, she nodded to the boy, who grinned back.

'*Adiós*,' he said to Sian and, his duty done, he ran back to join his companions.

Left alone with Señora Leiva, Sian shone a tentative smile. 'How did you come to learn English?' she enquired.

Leith, she thought wryly, would doubtless accuse her of wheedling out secrets again, but it seemed remarkable that someone from such a lacklustre background should be fluent, and she was intrigued.

'Because my daughter, Maria, married an Englishman and I hoped that one day I would have the chance to visit his country. However, it was not to be.' Her lined face had been solemn, but all of a sudden a sweet smile spread and the old lady's voice filled with pride. 'My daughter had a son, my grandson, and he came to see me three weeks ago for the very first time. He works as a journalist for an important newspaper in London.'

Sian stared. Life could toss out some extraordinary coincidences, but wasn't this stretching them too far? And yet, according to Alan, Leith's ancestry was Spanish. Like frantic express trains, thoughts shunted in and out of her head. *Only* according to Alan, she realised, for when she had repeated the assertion hadn't Leith said to remember that the grapevine was notorious for not getting its facts right?

'What's the paper called?' she asked.

'The *Vulcan*. You know of it?'

'Yes, yes,' Sian nodded, struggling to digest what she was being told.

Instead of being half-European-Spanish, Leith was half-Chilean-Spanish, and this old lady was his grandmother! But Maria Leiva had been an heiress—not just Alan, but Leith, too, had referred to her family's wealth—so how could a hovel on the outskirts of Santiago be explained? Had the Leiva fortunes taken a dramatic and drastic tumble? Was that why she had returned so abruptly to her homeland more than two decades ago and, filled with shame, could it be the reason why she had stayed? Latins were proud, stubborn people. Perhaps she had regarded the family's downfall as a personal disgrace?

'My daughter is dead for just two months,' the old lady continued sadly. 'Maria would have been overjoyed to have seen her son and to know what a tall, fine man he has become. He promised he would visit me again before he left, and I am very much looking forward to it. Though,' she added, with a wistful smile, 'I expected him to come back before now.'

Cold fingers clutched at Sian's heart. The only way Leith could return would be in a wheelchair. But shouldn't his grandmother be told what had happened and be given the chance to visit *him*? She hesitated. Whatever her own inclinations, this was his secret and she must respect it.

'When he learned Maria had died, my grandson was *un hombre torturado*,' Señora Leiva sighed, and then frowned, as though realising she was burdening a stranger with her sorrows. She tilted her silver head. 'May I help you in any way?' she queried courteously.

'No, thank you. I was just exploring and taking a few photographs,' Sian replied, and with a quick smile she hurried off.

Now she understood what had so absorbed Leith that he had blindly walked out into the road! Now she realised that in talking about 'going sooner' and 'leaving it too late' the reference had not been to jaywalking, but to seeing his mother. Now she knew why he had been continually wrapped up in his own thoughts. Distress grabbed her by the throat. After not seeing the woman he had mourned for all those years, it seemed unbearably poignant that Leith should miss her by a few short weeks!

The next day, the switch from hospital to the apart-hotel went smoothly. Leith had, he explained, spent the morning on a crash-course in how to manoeuvre a wheelchair and on arriving showed himself to be skilled. In minutes he had checked that the doorways were wide enough to allow clear passage from one room to another, and announced that he could manage.

'Thanks to my lumberjack's arms I can haul myself in and out of the wheelchair, in and out of bed, no problem,' he told her, his voice dry.

'Will they also enable you to reach up to the tap, fill the kettle, and make two cups of coffee?' Sian enquired pertly.

'No. Nor can I prepare meals,' he admitted, as she went into the kitchen alcove to start the procedure she had just described. 'However, if I hire a home-help along with the physiotherapist and nurse I'll be fine,' he added, a defiant edge to his voice.

Casting him a glance from beneath her lashes, Sian decided she agreed. Whether it was seeing him dressed again—he wore a black shirt and baggy beige slacks—or the Grand Prix manner in which he whizzed around, Leith gave every impression of a man determined to run his own life in his own way, and being capable of doing so. Plus, she thought with a flash of chagrin, and some pain, yet again he was spelling it out that her presence was superfluous!

'What did you do yesterday afternoon?' Leith questioned, when the coffee had been made.

'Yesterday afternoon?' Sian repeated, pretending to be engrossed in putting a plate of biscuits on the tray.

Straight-talking might be her natural style, but she had yet to decide whether or not to confess to what she had discovered. No matter how *relevant* it might seem, some things were sacred and she was uncertain about the ethics of intruding on such an intensely private and personal part of his life. Being confrontational was not always the answer. There were times for keeping quiet.

'Yes. Did Jill's mother cart you off to another museum? Or was it a case of "have camera, will take photographs"?'

'I took photographs.'

'Of what?'

'Boys kicking a ball, a few stray dogs, some kids playing house in a broken-down red Citroën,' she said, her tone determinedly casual.

'A broken-down red Citroën?' Leith repeated. His fingers clenched around the wooden arms of the wheelchair, their knuckles whitening. 'You went to Conchali!'

Hot colour ran up her face. What had made her garrulously describe the car? Sian wondered, and why must he be so acute? For a moment she was tempted to deny what had sounded like an accusation, but lying went against the grain and in any case—she cast him a wary look—she doubted he would believe her.

'You mentioned the place and I thought some photographs might be useful,' she said, walking across to set the tray down on a low table beside him.

Leith's eyes glittered. 'What else did you think might be useful?' he enquired.

Carefully, she placed the cups on saucers. 'I don't know what you mean.'

'No?' he jeered. 'How about a visit to my mother's home?'

'Your—your mother's home?' Sian repeated, and promptly cursed herself for such give-away stammering.

'You went there, didn't you? Didn't you?' he demanded.

'Yes, but——'

Fierce brown eyes nailed themselves to hers. 'I suppose you ferreted through my address book, then decided to stroll along and——'

Sian straightened, her chin lifting. She would not be intimidated. She refused to feel guilty. Her motives had been honourable and arrow-straight. 'Don't dump all your hostility on me,' she protested. 'I——'

'That wasn't hostility,' Leith rasped, '*this* is hostility. I never asked you to tamper in my affairs and I strongly resent it! And, if I wasn't bound to this damned wheelchair,' he said, slamming his palms down on the arms, 'I'd be sorely tempted to hit you!'

'I was trying to help.'

'I don't want any help!' Leith snarled, from the back of his throat.

'You might not want it, but you *need* it,' Sian retorted, and thrust a cup of coffee at him. 'You haven't moved your legs for a month and the medical profession swears your spine's intact, yet when counselling's suggested you——'

'I'm not talking to a bloody shrink!'

'The trouble with you is you won't talk to anyone!' she flared. 'You accuse me of being up-front—well, I'd far rather be honest and open than clutch everything furtively to my chest—like you! If something bothers me I say, I don't let it fester. OK, on the plane you managed to drop your guard and talk about personal things for a few minutes, though you seemed to instantly regret it——'

'I did!'

'—but ever since your accident you've been brooding—I assume about your mother—and where has it got you, what has it achieved? Damn-all! And you'll never achieve anything until you learn to *share*. Though,' Sian snapped, her eyes blazing, 'it's probably too late for that now.'

'You reckon?' Leith asked stiffly.

'I do, but in thinking you can go it alone, you're suffering from delusions of grandeur.'

His lip curled. 'I was wrong, you *did* major in psychology.'

She ignored him. 'Yes, I thought a visit to Conchali might be useful, though I didn't know how. All I knew was that I couldn't stand by and do *nothing*! When I read Maria Leiva's name it never occurred to me that she could be your mother. Why should it? All right, so there's a much-used sentence which begins "it's none of my business"; however——'

'It *is* none of your business!' Leith blasted.

Sian tugged at the collar of her silk shirt, drawing it closer around her neck. 'However,' she carried on, 'I went to Conchali not to attempt to derail you in some way, but with your well-being at heart. And it was by chance I met your grandmother.'

'You told her about my accident?' he demanded.

'No. I didn't admit to knowing you,' she said, and outlined what had happened and their conversation.

'Thanks for keeping quiet,' Leith muttered, and she saw that his anger was waning. 'Although my mother had apparently been ailing for years, when she died it came as one heck of a shock for the old lady, and so was seeing me. I don't want to land this——' a downward gesture indicated his inert legs '—on her, not yet.'

'She seemed a resilient kind of person; I'm sure she'd cope,' Sian protested. 'And she is expecting to see you again.'

'I know. I must decide what to do.'

'Presumably your grandmother is the reason why you want to remain in Chile?'

He nodded. 'I promised I'd visit her again and I intend to keep that promise, but I also need to work out how I can make life easier for her in the future.' Leith took a mouthful of coffee. 'My mother's death was one heck of a shock for me, too,' he muttered. 'If only Dot had found that folder earlier.'

'Which folder?'

He flung her a dark look and then he sighed. 'After my father died, Dot and I went through his papers,' he explained, grinding out the words in tight-lipped reluctance. 'We thought we'd covered the lot, but six weeks or so ago she was clearing out a desk and came across a folder which had become trapped at the back of a drawer. In it were a bundle of letters which my mother had written to me over the years, and each one carried the Conchali address.'

Sian sat down on the sofa. 'So she did try and get in touch!'

He nodded. 'Yet time and time again my father swore he'd never heard a word.'

'I wonder why he kept the letters?'

'I don't know. Maybe he had ideas of giving them to me on his deathbed? Though that was impossible because his coronary felled him in minutes.'

'Did they say why your mother's family had gone down in the world?' Sian enquired.

Leith's lips tightened. 'Gone down? They'd never been up.'

'But——'

'Oh, I'd always understood the Leivas were not just wealthy, but super-wealthy. My father told me they were—as he made a point of telling the rest of the world—and until the taxi deposited me in Conchali I believed him.' Harshly, he rubbed at his brow. 'I believed so much—for instance, my mother leaving because she wanted to.'

'She didn't?' Sian queried.

Leith shook his dark head. 'It was my father who ordered her to get the hell out of his life, and out of mine.'

CHAPTER SEVEN

'HE WASN'T the injured party?' Sian asked, in surprise.

Leith's lower lip stiffened into a downward slant of disgust. 'He was the *injurer*, and with a vengeance!'

'But what happened? Why did he send your mother away?'

Leith gulped down another mouthful of coffee, and when he started to speak again it was willingly. 'He kicked her out because he felt she was stifling his social ambitions—a cardinal sin in his book. From the moment he dismissed her until almost thirty years later when he died he persistently fed me lies and I never had the wit to realise.' His eyes burned with anger and remorse. 'I was a damned fool!'

'You couldn't have realised,' she protested. 'You were only a child when your mother disappeared so——'

'I may not have known much about her, but I knew what *he* was like,' he cut in. 'I've been rethinking my life and, Sian, there were so many clues!'

'This is why you've been distracted?'

'To begin with, yes. My father's innocence had been a basic belief and an integral factor in our relationship—I'd always felt sorry for him because he'd been spurned!—so to discover he was the villain of the piece totally bombed me out. It took time to get a grip on things again.' Leith's brow furrowed. 'I've repeated so many past conversations, re-enacted so many scenes in my head, been forced to make all manner of adjustments. I knew my parents had met when my father's bank sent him to Chile to negotiate a series of international loans, but what I didn't know was that my mother worked as a receptionist at the hotel where he stayed on his various trips. He'd always maintained he'd been introduced to her at some upper-crust cocktail party.'

'He was aware she came from a humble background?' Sian enquired.

'Yes, though he never went near Conchali.'

'Why not? Didn't your mother want him to see how she lived?'

'She wasn't proud of her home, but she didn't feel embarrassed by it, either. Nor should she have been. Her father had died in a factory fire when she was tiny and yet although it had been a struggle for Filomena to raise her and her brothers, they'd managed.'

'You have uncles?' Sian said.

'Three, and each is married so there are aunts and a whole tribe of cousins whom I've never met. My mother would have been pleased to welcome him into her home,' Leith continued, 'and he was invited, but it seems he always made excuses. My grandmother said that on the few occasions when she met my father it was at the hotel. I suspect he'd realised Maria Leiva came from somewhere near the bottom of the pile, but preferred not to know. If he didn't see the reality, he could pretend it didn't exist. Pretence appears to have been his forte,' he remarked blisteringly. 'However, in the first flush of love it was enough that she looked like an angel, so he took her back to England and married her.'

'And claimed she was an heiress?'

'Yes. What you need to understand is that my father was a devout social Sherpa. He spent his entire adult life positioning himself for a knighthood and when, after years of studiously being in the right place, doing all the right things, it finally happened, he believed he'd reached the zenith. Status was his god. He would never have admitted to a working wife with nothing in the way of family background, because that wouldn't have impressed anybody, and to own up to a wife who was working-class—that would have been a fate worse than death!'

Sian frowned. 'But your mother must have gone along with the deception.'

Leith nodded. 'As, at first, he was pole-axed by her looks, so she was apparently overwhelmed with love for this take-charge banker who was so well-versed in the demands of society, as he saw them.'

'And so she made no objections?'

'It seems as though whatever Charles said went,' he agreed. 'Don't forget that, while my father had a domineering streak, my mother was a shy, mild-tempered woman. Add the fact that she was an alien in a foreign country and dependent on her husband for everything, and I guess resisting him couldn't have been easy.' Abruptly Leith's mouth indented at one corner. 'She wasn't a member of the lay-it-on-the-line, slug-it-out, stand-up-for-herself brigade, like you. That's a compliment,' he said, when Sian cast him a look.

'It is?' she said dubiously.

'Yes. Anyhow, apparently not too many months passed by before my grandmother began to receive letters bemoaning the fact that my father was attempting to tutor his wife in social chitchat and how to cultivate useful people, and that no matter how hard she tried he was never satisfied. Sounds in character,' he commented cryptically. 'Although he was fond of Dot, I'm sure he married her because she came with all the proper contacts, all the proper friends, and was a wow at getting invited to high-spots on the social calendar, like Ascot and Henley and the opera at Glyndebourne. But my mother didn't much care for parties and found hostessing hard going.' Leith rubbed at his brow again. 'I suspect that if she hadn't become pregnant my father would have kicked her back to Chile much sooner—but she did, and he wanted a son. I was the one thing poor Maria Leiva managed to get right!'

'And presumably you were the reason she survived as long as she did? It's noticeable that the minute you were old enough to be sent away to school she was sent packing,' Sian defined.

He nodded. 'I suppose there are those who would claim it was to my father's credit that he let her stick around until I'd reached boyhood, but when it came to discarding her the bastard showed no compassion. None!' Leith shot her a glance. 'I realise you might see a similarity between my father and me when— when I've tried to discard you,' he faltered, 'but——'

'Our relationship doesn't include marriage and a child,' she dismissed quickly, having no wish to divert to that topic now.

'No,' he muttered, and momentarily fell silent. 'Filomena told me that when I went away to school my mother was broken-hearted,' he carried on, 'and so, supposedly to comfort her, my father arranged for her to visit Chile. She'd been a couple of times since her marriage, though he'd never allowed her to take me; presumably because even though I was small I'd have realised her family weren't bloated pluto- crats and given the game away,' Leith said pun- gently. 'However, as they were driving to the airport Charles revealed that the ticket he'd bought her was one-way, that he had begun divorce proceedings, and that he expected her to relinquish all rights to her son.'

'He waited until she was on the point of de- parture before he dumped all that on her?' Sian protested, in horror.

'It's called perfect timing,' Leith grated. 'He informed her the differences between her world and his were too wide to bridge, and that with her shyness and lack of social nous she was a liability, both to him and to me.' Leith bowed his head to his chest, and when he raised it again his eyes were misty. 'How could he take away her marriage, her child and then trample over her self-esteem?' he demanded.

'Your mother still went along with his wishes?' Sian enquired.

'No—at last she rebelled. She told him he could have his divorce, but she wanted her son.'

'And?' she prompted softly, when he lowered his head again.

'He said his lawyers had assured him that a court would never allow her to remove me from a settled, comfortable home in England to take pot luck in a slum in Chile. Whether that was correct or not, who knows?'

'But she flew back to Santiago?'

Leith pinched the bridge of his nose with his fingertips. 'Yes. My grandmother said she only boarded the plane because she was in shock and didn't know what else to do, and that she fully intended to return. However, within days my father was bombarding her with divorce papers and letters reiterating what he'd already said. He told her that if she tried to claim me he'd use everything in his power to stop her and, compared to hers, his power was considerable. If it had been possible she would have hired her own lawyers and fought back, but my father had made sure she had access to only a modest amount of cash. Virtually all she took away from seven years of marriage were two suitcases of clothes and a few pieces of jewellery.' He let out a melancholy breath. 'She sold the jewellery to finance her journey back to England, but soon afterwards she fell ill and the money was soaked up in doctor's bills.'

Sian frowned. 'You said your mother was ailing for years?'

'That's right. Filomena reckoned she was never very strong, and that the distress she suffered dragged her down physically and played havoc with her nerves. It seems my father managed to ruin her health, in addition to every other part of her life,' Leith said scathingly.

'It's so sad to think that she continually wrote you letters.'

'Apparently each one was sent with the fervent prayer it would be the one which received an answer, and yet my father diverted them all.' His jaw tightened. 'There was quite a bundle, so it must have taken some doing.'

'As must living a lie all those years,' Sian pointed out.

'I guess.'

For a minute or two they were both silent, lost in their thoughts.

'So Señora Leiva went to all the trouble of learning English, but never did get to England,' she remarked wistfully.

Leith came back to life. 'That's what makes the whole thing so...shoddy!' he rasped, brandishing an arm. 'The Leivas may not have too many *pesos* to rub together, but so what? They're clean and decent. They believe in education. They're triers. They're not people to be ashamed of!'

'But when your father refused to speak about your mother it was because he was ashamed— of himself,' Sian reflected.

'And so he needed to be!' Leith swore virulently. 'How could anyone have been such a——?'

'Slimeball?' she inserted, when he seemed lost for a word.

'Exactly,' he agreed, his tone dry. 'You ought to be the writer, your vocabulary is far more colourful than mine.' He drained his cup and reached down to place it on the table. 'There,' he said, with a sudden grin, 'that wasn't so bad, was it?'

'Sorry?'

'This afternoon I've stopped clutching everything to my chest and talked about it—and the sun hasn't fallen out of the sky. Not yet. Mind you, neither am I about to shout "Eureka!", leap out of this wheelchair, and perform a fandango,' Leith continued. 'That is what baring my soul is intended to achieve, o, my therapist?'

'I was thinking more in terms of a quick snatch of break-dancing.' Sian smiled, then her expression sobered. 'You said the situation with your parents had absorbed you—but only at first?'

He nodded. 'I realise it sounds crazy, but immediately after the accident I had tunnel vision and it was all I could focus on. My injuries hurt like hell, yet they didn't matter. I didn't care. I even felt that getting smashed up and being paralysed was no more than I deserved.'

She stared at him in dismay. 'For heaven's sake, why?' she demanded.

'It seemed like I needed to be punished for not trying to contact my mother much earlier.'

'But you thought she'd walked out on you,' Sian protested.

'I know, and gradually I acknowledged that fact and stopped blaming myself.' He moistened his lips. 'But once the agonising over my mother ended, I was then faced with a life which has caved in, with a career which has been halted, with legs which won't bloody well function! Unlike you, I don't believe there's a magic wand somewhere waiting to be waved, so I've been attempting to confront what's happened and come to terms with it. Not easy.' Leith gave a twisted smile. 'However,' he went on quickly, 'if you'll excuse me I'll go and lie down. One way and another today's been quite eventful and all of a sudden I feel whacked.' As Sian made to help him, he lifted a hand. 'Thanks, but I'm OK.'

For a split second she hesitated, then she nodded. 'I'll clear the coffee things away.'

As she took the tray into the kitchen, Leith wheeled himself through to the bedroom. Maybe he was right about there being no magic wand, Sian thought unhappily as she started the washing-up. Maybe he would be paralysed forever. She so much wanted to be optimistic and believe in Doctor Mardones' theory, and yet time was passing and nothing was changing and . . .

A muttering, followed by a selection of oaths, interrupted her thoughts.

'Everything all right?' she called.

There was some more swearing, silence, and eventually Leith yelled, 'No.'

Drying her hands, Sian went through to find him perched on the edge of the bed with the wheelchair out of reach.

'Don't ask me how, but I managed to push the damn thing away and now, if I try to move, I'm in danger of sliding on to the floor,' he grumbled disgustedly.

She assessed the situation. 'If I lift from behind and you push up on your arms, between us we should be able to manoeuvre you further on to the bed. Then you'll be able to swivel around and lie down.' Kneeling at the back of him, Sian hooked her arms around his chest and heaved—shuffling backwards as he also shuffled. 'Easy,' she said, grinning, a minute later.

Her grin was fake. Leith's lower limbs might be inoperative, but he remained a firm-bodied male with considerable powers of attraction, and manhandling him had brought thoughts of the last time they had been on a bed together unbidden into her mind. It was a bitter-sweet memory.

'Thanks. Before we go any further, do you think you could straighten this?' he asked, frowning at the bedspread which had become crumpled beneath him. 'If I lift myself up again, you should be able to manage.'

Every inch the efficient automaton, Sian came back round the bed and stationed herself beside him, bent ready to tug. 'Lift away,' she instructed.

Leith was in the midst of raising himself when the mattress unexpectedly dipped to one side and, hand skidding and elbow bending, he started to topple away. Sian lunged. He caught at her arm. She was yanked off balance.

'Oh!' she squeaked, as he fell back amid the pillows with her locked on top of him.

How had it happened? Leith had needed to grab, but had he needed to grab quite so determinedly? Had he needed to wrench her off her feet? Was she spreadeagled on top of him by accident or design? Sian decided she knew the answer when she attempted to move, and his arms tightened around her.

'I'm squashing your legs,' she protested.

'My legs are fine,' Leith replied, smiling up into the flushed face which was only inches above his, 'and now that you've flattened me, this seems the ideal time to embark on some serious grovelling. I want to apologise for losing my temper earlier, and at the hospital. I deeply regret it, Sian. Sometimes I blow my stack when I'm worried and that's what happened.'

'Apology accepted,' she told him briskly. 'Now let's see if we can sort out the bedspread.'

Yet although she squirmed for freedom, Leith refused to release her. Sian lay rigid on top of him. Just the two thin layers of clothes separated them, and squirming was having an alarming effect on her composure, on the heat of her skin, on her breasts.

'There's more,' he went on. 'I also want to thank you for helping me today and for all the other help you've provided.'

'You've thanked me before,' she protested, and attempted to extricate herself again—in vain.

'Maybe, but you've done so much,' he said, his voice husky with sincerity. 'Sian, you've kept me safe and sane, and I'll be forever grateful. I could never have survived without you.'

She flashed a quick smile. 'You would have got by.'

'I doubt it.' Leith raised his fingers and tenderly brushed a wisp of pale flame from her brow. 'Thank God for tough butterflies—*my* tough butterfly,' he murmured, and his hand moved to the back of her head. 'Undo it,' he implored, tugging gently at the burnished plait which hung there. 'Release your hair and let it fall around your shoulders. You have beautiful hair, Sian. Beautiful shoulders. All of you is beautiful.' His fingers caressed the soft skin of her cheek. 'And you're beautiful to touch.'

Her heart fluttered in the cage of her ribs. 'Leith,' she protested.

For a tense, silent, stretching moment he gazed deep into her eyes, and then he grinned, fracturing the mood. 'You're right, we must stop meeting like this,' he said.

Happy now to match him, Sian pulled a pained face. 'Where do you get your gift for cliché? Surely, Mr Journalist, you can come up with something better?'

Leith frowned. 'As a matter of fact, I can,' he said, and, spreading his hands on her hips, he slid her against him.

'Oh,' Sian gasped again, every nerve and fibre sensitive to the masculine thrust of the body beneath hers.

'You didn't realise I could still become aroused? Neither did I, and it's one heck of a relief.' He gave a strangled laugh. 'No, it isn't. Not at all. It's... *hell*! Go,' he ordered, and pushed her from him.

She scrambled upright. 'Leith, if—er—if that can happen,' she said awkwardly, 'doesn't it mean——'

'Would you sling a couple of pillows in behind me?' he interrupted, and pushed himself into a sitting position. 'Thanks. Maybe I should get a second opinion,' he muttered.

In the living-room, the intercom buzzed.

'You should,' Sian told him, and went to answer it. 'The physiotherapist is downstairs,' she called, a moment or two later. 'She knows she wasn't supposed to come until tomorrow, but a couple of her appointments have been cancelled back-to-back and she wonders if she could start you off with a monster session now? You said the hospital physio reckoned you couldn't have too much work done on your legs,' she reminded him, when he did not reply. 'And, who knows, she might be able to give you a few tips on getting into bed on your own,' Sian added crisply.

There was a pause. 'OK,' Leith agreed, and she passed on the affirmative.

'She's on her way up,' she informed him, coming back into the bedroom. 'She'll be here for roughly an hour and a half, and, lucky you, the lady speaks some English.' Sian stuck her hands in her trouser pockets and frowned. Leith's friskiness had taken her unawares and unprepared, and now some solitary thinking was urgently required. 'As you'll be busy I'll go for a walk,' she decided.

'If you do you could get soaked.'

Swivelling, she gazed in surprise at the dark clouds which were gathering. Not much earlier it had been sunny and clear, but with so much going on indoors she had been oblivious to what had been happening outside.

'Then I'll go to the cinema.'

'The cinema?' Leith protested.

She nodded. 'It isn't far and I can take my umbrella. A horror film's showing, an American one with subtitles,' Sian told him, hurriedly recalling the posters. 'It had terrific write-ups and I've been desperate to see it for months.'

He shot her a sceptical look. 'I never realised you were hooked on green slime and graphic scenes of disembowelment.'

'They're fun,' she assured him, with a brilliant smile, then bit into the side of her lip. 'It's possible the physiotherapist may go before I'm back. Will you——?'

Leith wafted a hand. 'Don't worry about me,' he said.

Sian found her way along a row in the stalls and sat down. Her thinking would be *very* solitary, she acknowledged, as she glanced around. In mid-afternoon and mid-week, the cinema was almost empty. Through the flickering darkness, all she could see were half a dozen popcorn-eating children in the front seats and, at the back, a teenage couple conjoined in an ardent embrace.

By chance, her arrival had coincided with the advertisements at the start of the programme, and as the buy-me delights of branded jeans and lager and cola were extolled, Sian got busy with the task in hand. She had coped with Leith's aloofness and his anger, but by opening up to her this afternoon—which was a victory she had pushed for!—he had brought them back around to friendship. She doubted she could handle that, not again. And, to complicate matters, his 'wicked crush' appeared to have been revived. Leith might no longer be able to make chase and straddle her on the bed, she thought with a frown, yet he remained capable of seducing her in other less tactile, though ultimately more heart-devouring, soul-destroying ways. Sian sighed. Before she had trodden a dangerously fine line between falling in love and falling flat on her face, and had escaped both—just. But she had no intention of risking a repeat of either calamity at this stage in the game!

Ruminatively she chewed at a thumbnail. Perhaps she had not escaped? Perhaps that was self-delusion and all she had done was bury her feelings for him alive? Perhaps Leith had skewered her, for now and forever? Sian lost patience. Forget theories. Scrap wondering. Whatever, the bottom line was the same—she must go. It was true his physical condition had not changed since she had fought so strenuously against leaving before, and the thought of walking out on an invalid still caused unease, but if she went his emotional equilibrium would happily survive, whereas if she remained hers could be irreparably damaged.

The destruction of her thumbnail continued. Leith had said not to worry about him but, of course, she did, and although her gut feeling was to leave *now*, it was impossible. He might have claimed that, courtesy of home-help, physiotherapist and part-time nurse, he could manage, but one hour in the apartment had shown otherwise. Someone was needed to constantly watch out for him. Someone who could, if necessary, haul him around. She frowned. The solution would be to combine the roles of home-help and nurse in the form of a personal assistant, though locating a suitable English-speaking person could take time. So be it—but the day someone was engaged would be the day she left.

Sian mapped out a plan of action. One, she would give notice of her intention to leave and suggest an assistant. Surely Leith would agree? Two, she would locate the appropriate employment agencies and do the rounds. Three, she would make sure that even if the two of them did come into bodily contact again—and it seemed inevitable—no intimacy would be allowed to develop.

The wail of violins indicated the start of the main film, and Sian turned her attention to the screen. Her solitary thinking had culminated in a trio of firm decisions, so she might as well watch and be terrified!

For the next hour, the hair repeatedly stood up on the back of her neck. One of the better of the genre, the film used its frightening moments sparingly and with skin-shivering impact. The heroine entered a deserted log cabin. A

tape recorder played mysterious messages.
Hands burst through doors and tried to dig
themselves out of graves. As the children in the
front row shrieked and screamed, Sian found
her fingers flying to her throat and gooseflesh
chilling her arms. The soundtrack was particularly good. Noise crept up from all angles, so
that it seemed as if the creaks and whispers and
thuds were happening around her.

All of a sudden, the floor beneath her feet
gave a slight shudder. She looked down in surprise. Had it been her imagination? She had
heard of films which incorporated special ef-
fects within the cinema and it struck her that
the apparent movement might be one. A minute
or two later, the screen rippled. Sian frowned.
This did not heighten the horror; on the contrary, it distracted. Had the ripple been on
purpose? Whether or not, the kids were still
yelling and the couple on the back row continued to neck.

Sian was absorbed in the film again when a
voice rang out above in the circle. She tilted an
ear. Someone was making an impatient and
flat-voiced announcement. It was impossible
to hear what they said, but seconds later emp-
tying seats thumped as the few patrons apparently departed. Had the screen developed a
fault? Was the show being cancelled? Not much
later, the doors at the back of the stalls swung
open and an usherette appeared to repeat the

same message she had recited before. Sian listened hard, but the heroine had begun to scream and the only word which emerged from the cacophony was *'terremoto'*. What did it mean? As the usherette backed out and the doors crashed shut, her heart gave a sudden lurch. *Terremoto,* she had remembered, was Spanish for earthquake!

Sian rose to her feet. The children jumped up. The teenage couple sprang apart. Everyone had begun heading for the aisle when the screen went dark and the cinema was plunged into what, for an instant, seemed like total blackness. A little girl started to cry. Sian blinked, her eyes adjusting to the gloom, then felt and fumbled her way to the end of the row. At the rear of the cinema, twin squares of bright light shone like beacons through the windows in the swing-doors and she walked thankfully towards them.

Her thanks were short-lived. The young couple had arrived first, and when she and the children came up they found the youth tugging determinedly at the handles—but the doors refused to open.

'Terremoto?' one of the boys queried, but the youth shook his head and told him that the doors had not been jammed through any earth movement, but were locked. What must have happened, he said, was that when the usherette

had left they had banged shut and the catch had been sprung.

The little girl was still crying and Sian bent to comfort her. A minute ago she had been frightened herself, but her nerves were rapidly steadying. The earthquake had been no more than a tremor; like the one her friend, Jill, had experienced, and which she had also said were not uncommon. There was no need to panic. The usherette's announcement had, she recalled, been one of irritation not distress, and there had been a single shudder of the floor, one ripple of the screen. Doubtless the building had been cleared to comply with some cautionary regulation. She looked back into the darkness. The cinema was old and solidly built. It would have successfully withstood far more severe quakes.

The youth had begun thumping at the door when a face peered in. It was the usherette. A high-decibel conversation followed which, as far as Sian could follow, consisted of the woman asking what was the problem, the youth explaining, and her grumbling about the faulty catch and promising to bring a key.

'Pronto,' Sian said, with a gesture to indicate the doors would soon be opened, and the little girl stopped crying.

But it was five minutes before the usherette arrived back with a bunch of keys and then, although she laboriously tried each one, none would fit. By now, the little girl and her pals were growing bored, and, as the woman went off again, they began playing tag up and down the aisle. The youth and his girlfriend also drifted away, to see whether either of the side doors were open. As Sian waited alone, a bearded man, whom she assumed to be the manager, arrived to shout apologies, and various other people looked in through the tiny windows. By the time the usherette returned, a small crowd seemed to have gathered. Maybe they were the children's mothers and fathers?

Again the woman wielded a bunch of keys and again she began the ritual of experiment. The teenage couple wandered back with the news of no other exit, and the children stopped playing and came to wait. One key was tried. And another. And another. Out of the blue, Sian remembered her umbrella. She had left it under her seat. Back down the aisle she went, into the gloom. The row she had occupied had been roughly halfway on the left and the seat had been halfway along the row. But which row? Eagle-eyed, she hiked down one, re-turned via the next, and hiked again. There was her umbrella, half hidden beneath a seat! Sian was crouched down to retrieve it, when sud-denly she heard a crash at the back of the audi-torium and the doors burst open.

'Sian!' a voice thundered in desperation. 'Sian, where are you?'

Kneeling, she peered over the top of the seats. Silhouetted by the light, she saw a tall, broad-shouldered man making his way down the aisle. He was walking unevenly, but unaided. Sian gazed at him with widened, wondering eyes.

'Leith!' she exclaimed. 'Oh, Leith,' and she began to cry.

CHAPTER EIGHT

A BOTTLE of champagne clutched in each fist and a wide smile on his face, Doctor Mardones walked into the apartment. 'I was dining at a nearby restaurant when your message reached me,' he explained, presenting his cargo to Sian, 'and rather than wait until the morning to offer my congratulations I decided to call in now.' He patted Leith on the back and vigorously shook his hand. 'It's great to have you standing tall again—though,' he said, looking up at his six feet three inches, 'I never realised you were quite *so* tall.'

Laughing, his ex-patient thanked him for his gift and his good wishes. 'People who say "I told you so" usually drive me wild, but please,' Leith told him wryly, 'be my guest.'

'My only observation is that when I said some kind of a shock was needed to get you moving again, I never meant it literally! So— what happened?'

'First let's open the champagne,' Leith suggested.

'Not for me. I've already had a couple of glasses of wine and I'm driving.' Hazel eyes twinkled behind steel-rimmed spectacles. 'Even so, I can't stay long—there's a luscious brunette waiting for me in the car.'

Leith grinned. 'Then Sian and I will have a drink later, and I'll talk quickly. I'd better sit down quickly, too,' he added, reaching for a chair. 'My legs feel as if they're made of foam rubber.'

'It will be ten days or so before they're back to full strength,' the doctor told him.

Waiting until everyone was seated, Leith started on his tale. 'This afternoon the windows suddenly rattled and the next minute the entire apartment block appeared to sway.'

'These multi-storey buildings can move by as much as a metre at the top, and the higher you are the more you feel it.' The younger man shrugged. 'But they're built to withstand quakes and most times there's no damage.'

'The porter said there wasn't any damage here today,' Sian confirmed.

'Maybe,' Leith agreed, 'and maybe the building steadied and it was all over, but I got one hell of a scare. However, what disturbed me more was the thought of what might have happened to Sian. She'd gone down the road to see a film,' he said, and explained how the physiotherapist had called. 'I remembered the cinema was a big, stone, archaic-looking building and I had visions of its collapsing and her being trapped.' A vein pulsed in his temple. 'I knew I had to get over there, and fast.'

Doctor Mardones frowned. 'You went down in the elevator?'

'There was no alternative.'

'You realise it's extremely dangerous to use them at such times?'

'The lift was vital,' Leith said impatiently. 'Even if I could have bumped down twelve flights of stairs on my backside, it would have taken forever and I'd still have needed the wheelchair at the end of it. When I got outside I set off down the road, and——' he grimaced at his hands '—almost wore my palms away propelling the wheelchair along. Twice I was on the brink of tipping over and once a truck nearly ran me down when I was crossing a road.'

Sian stared in horror. Earlier, when he had described his journey, he had omitted to tell her that. 'Again?' she protested.

'It missed me. I steamrollered up kerbs and down kerbs, and eventually reached the cinema—where I was confronted by a flight of stone steps.' Leith blew out a breath. 'I'd forgotten about them.'

'Consternation?' suggested the doctor.

'Blue funk,' he replied pithily. 'I could see no sign of any destruction, but a group of people were gathered inside so it was obvious something was wrong.' He cast Sian a glance. 'To speak in cliché, I found myself at the top of the steps before I realised what had happened. As I staggered through the foyer a woman was fiddling with the swing-doors into the stalls and it seemed as if Sian might be inside, so I gave the doors a massive push and kept on going.' His mouth curved in memory. 'I found her crouched down between the seats—safe and sound.'

'She would be. Those old buildings are sturdy,' Doctor Mardones told him. 'I assume there was minimal structural damage?'

Leith frowned. 'I didn't notice. How much of a knock did the cinema take?' he asked Sian.

'None.'

'No cracks appeared in the walls and no plaster fell down?' he demanded.

She shook her head. 'As far as I'm aware, the building was completely unharmed.'

'In that case,' he said, his frown deepening, 'why——?'

'Today's reading on the Richter scale was low, so I expect you barely noticed the quake?' the doctor butted in, speaking to Sian.

She hesitated.

'Of course she noticed it,' Leith protested. 'She was terrified. It took her a full half an hour to stop crying.'

The visitor shot her a quick look. 'And when you found her, you fell at her feet?' he enquired.

'I crumpled like tissue paper,' Leith agreed, sketching the motion with a vivid movement of his fingers. 'How did you guess?'

'Stands to reason that once the motivation was removed, legs which had been inactive for so long would feel the strain and buckle,' came the matter-of-fact reply. 'Now, would you care to walk to the door and back a couple of times and allow me to assess your current capability?'

As Leith went shakily through his paces, Doctor Mardones thrust her another sidelong glance. Sian kept her gaze fixed ahead. What he had also correctly diagnosed—and what the erstwhile invalid had failed to realise—was the cause for *all* her crying. While her initial sobbed-out relief and delight had clearly had much to do with seeing him walk again, when her weeping had continued Leith had blamed the strain and stresses of the earthquake. It had been an erroneous conclusion, but Sian had not enlightened him. After all, if she confessed to uncontrollable crying over him, she would be confessing to a whole lot more.

'I understand you have a pool here,' Doctor Mardones said, as Leith's parading ended, 'so have a swim every day. But exercise gently, don't rush, and if you feel tired lie down. I'd like to see you in a week's time,' he grinned, 'just to gloat. And now——' his grin stretched '—it's time I returned to my brunette.'

As Sian rose and joined the two men at the door, Leith slung an arm around her shoulders.

'Thanks for coming this evening,' he told their visitor. 'We appreciate it.' After a smiling exchange of goodbyes, the doctor departed. 'Champagne?' Leith suggested.

'Please.' Dipping out of his embrace, Sian passed him a bottle. The cork popped, foam spurted, pale yellow liquid bubbled and sparkled in crystal glasses. *'Salud!'* she said.

'Salud!' He grinned.

Sitting in the corner of the sofa, she slipped off her shoes and folded her blue-denimed legs beneath her. Thoughtfully, Sian sipped her champagne. The way Leith had put his arm around her had not only been too familiar for comfort, it indicated that her need to get away had become more crucial than ever. She ran her fingers slowly up and down the stem of the glass. She must run, get out, and with him self-sufficient again there was nothing to stop her. As soon as she could she would book a flight—maybe tomorrow?

'We've forgotten to ring London!' she said suddenly.

'In all the excitement, you're surprised?' Leith checked the steel and gold watch on his wrist. 'It's too late now, but I'll speak to Giles in the morning. I'll tell him he can expect us back in—what, three weeks? That'll give me time to recover and sort things out with my grandmother, and allow us to complete our assignment.'

'I've completed my part,' Sian said. 'I've taken plenty of photographs, so whatever you write there will be something which will fit. I've already been here far longer than I expected and another three weeks is too much,' she insisted, when he opened his mouth to protest. 'You don't need me any more, so——'

'I do need you,' Leith interjected, 'and we need to discuss what's going to happen with us.'

Us? The word was emotive and his husky pronunciation made it more so, yet Sian refused to be deceived. He might have been inspired to rescue her—as he thought—but she saw no reason to endow the act with significant meaning. He was a responsible human being—he would have been inspired to rescue anyone.

'There's no such thing as "us",' she said, defiantly shaking her head. 'All we have is a working relationship.'

'To use your word—twaddle!'

'It's true.' She frowned. 'You may think you—you quite like me, but——'

'Just quite?' Leith protested.

'—but that's very much linked to your gratitude for my help at a time of trouble.'

'Complete and utter——' This time 'twaddle' was replaced by an obscenity.

'I don't deny that your accident has brought us together in various ways,' Sian continued, regardless, 'but the reality is that we're work colleagues, I'm not interested in an affair, and—and you have a girlfriend. One whom you haven't bothered to contact for over three weeks!' she ended astringently.

'That's because she doesn't exist.'

'Excuse me?'

Leith lifted the bottle from the low table and replenished their drinks. 'I don't have a girlfriend,' he said.

Sian straightened her back. 'You mean you deliberately lied?' she demanded.

'Don't sound so outraged,' he said, cradling his glass in his fingers. 'You've lied to me.'

'When?' she protested. 'What about?'

'Today. About your crying jag.'

She flicked her plait from her shoulder. 'I did not!'

'Maybe you didn't actually say the earthquake was your sole reason for being so upset,' Leith retorted, sinking down at the other end of the sofa, his long legs stretched out before him, 'but that's what you encouraged me to believe. Be honest, did you feel anything of the tremor at the cinema?'

'The floor juddered and the screen shook,' she mumbled.

'For how long?'

'A second or two.'

'And that was all?' She bobbed her head. 'So why was a crowd clustered in the foyer?' he enquired.

Sian took a sustaining mouthful of champagne. 'The doors had become locked by mistake and there was some delay finding a key.'

'And I barged in there ready to shoulder beams, break down walls with my bare hands, and save you from certain death. Hail the conquering fool!' Leith said drily. 'Then, like a fool, I misinterpreted all the weeping as you pushed me back along the road. Your tears were over me, weren't they?' he demanded. 'Every single one!'

Sian's colour rose. 'I was pleased you could walk. Pleased the paralysis had gone. It—it was a natural reaction,' she replied jerkily. She knew there must be stronger threads to be woven into her argument, but found it impossible to think of any. 'Plus or minus a girlfriend doesn't change anything,' she hurried on. 'You see, I also believe that conducting a personal relationship within a work situation is fraught with problems and better avoided.'

He thrust her a sharp look. 'Since when?'

'Since I thought about what you said,' she declared stalwartly.

'You know why I said it? Because I was scared stiff of becoming involved—which, I suspect, could have something to do with why you're saying it now.' Jettisoning his glass, Leith sat forward, his hands clasped between his knees. 'It's been well over a year since I've dated anyone and that's been for two reasons.'

Sian regarded him with wary eyes. His attitude made it plain he was planning on being honest and open again, but if that happened wasn't there a danger that she might, in turn, find herself being pushed into confidences, too? She frowned. Her inclination to enter the revealing-all arena was zero. 'It's gone ten o'clock and you must be tired,' she protested. 'Let's leave this for now.'

'I thought you were the great advocate for talking?' Leith demanded.

'In certain circumstances, but——'

'I want to talk,' he declared. 'One reason for my steering clear of involvements was my track record. For a long time now I've been highly sensitive to my inability to sustain a relationship, and it bothered the hell out of me. I was even beginning to wonder whether I possessed

the capacity to love. When a break-up occured,
I went through agonies wondering why, wondering whether it had been inevitable, wondering how much of it was my fault and
suspecting that the answer could be "most".
Admitting to personal defects is not easy——'
his mouth twisted into the mockery of a smile
'—but I'll get back to that later. The second
reason why my socialising ground to a halt was
you.'

Sian's eyes opened wide. She had decided she
would make no comment and thus—hopefully—he would grow weary of his monologue,
but this claim hooked her. 'Me?' she asked.

'It was ages before I realised it myself, but
after we'd been together in Afghanistan I
started to be critical of other women. Some
female would sidle up and almost subconsciously I'd start comparing her with you, and
two seconds later I'd conclude she wasn't worth
knowing. You see, until we met I'd never had
a woman as a friend.'

She sent a doubtful look along the sofa.
'No?'

'No. I've been out with some very pleasant
girls, but there was always a gap which separated us. Sometimes a narrow one, but a gap
none the less. There wasn't with you. We met,
slotted into a relationship almost without my
noticing it, and proceeded to have a straight-

forward *great* time. We were interested in the same things, we laughed at the same things, we were on the same wavelength. It was the much-flaunted togetherness—albeit platonic.' Leith gave a faint smile. 'Then, a couple of months ago, it dawned on me that I was becoming seriously attached to you and I very much wanted to go to bed with you, and that messed up everything. It reminded me that, sooner or later, all my other liaisons had ended and the thought of our ending—well, it was the last thing I wanted. So I decided that if I was to preserve our relationship it must remain static, and that meant avoiding any sexual content like the plague.' He gave a dry laugh. 'When you arrived hot-foot at my flat that day, it threw me.'

Sian's brow creased. 'I thought you were annoyed because I'd interrupted your work?'

'No, what upset me was having you in my home. As long as you were restricted to a work environment, even abroad, I felt we were safe,' he explained, 'but once you entered my personal space it seemed as if you were advancing our relationship and...inside me, all hell broke loose. Your determination to come to Chile made it worse,' Leith sighed. 'I tried gentle persuasion but you weren't receptive, and so I saw no alternative but to be blunt.'

'As in sledgehammer.'

Rueful brown eyes met hers. 'If it's any consolation, I didn't sleep a wink that night for worrying about what I'd done.'

'Good,' Sian said succinctly. 'And you'd suggested the assignment to Giles Summerton because you wanted to visit your mother?' she asked.

'Anything I write will be of interest in so much as the country *is* interesting, so the assignment is of value professionally—but yes. Giles made a general reference to Latin America during one of our what-comes-next discussions, and I saw a chance and promoted Chile. After twenty-odd years, it seemed that at last I'd tracked down my mother, so if there was an opportunity to meet her I intended to take it. I know I could have waited until my leave later in the year, but I was too impatient.'

She flashed him a sympathetic smile. 'And yet you were still too late.'

'Unfortunately.' Leith brooded for a moment. 'When I said I hadn't wanted you with me because I was frightened of our relationship running out of control, it was true—but I had another reason.'

'My ant-eater's nose?' Sian enquired.

He laughed. 'Got it in one. I felt threatened by your flair for discovering what's going on around you and I wanted to keep any meeting with my mother a secret.' He grimaced. 'I arrived at Heathrow keyed-up and very excited, though I had no idea what I'd say when eventually I met her, but then, when you appeared, I found myself forced to acquire an ultra-cool persona. It wasn't the simplest thing I've ever done.'

'You didn't quite make it. Those million and one questions when we landed were something of a give-away.'

Leith grinned. 'My tension wasn't *all* to do with you. Being in the country of my ancestors was gripping stuff, too.'

'I don't understand why keeping your mother under wraps mattered so much,' Sian said, frowning. 'I wouldn't have interfered.'

'I know, I know, but keeping quiet had nothing to do with you and everything to do with me. Or, to be more exact, with my unwillingness to share; which brings me back to my past. Your theory about the relationship with the mother being at the root of all relationships could have some validity,' he mused, 'but——'

She shook her head. 'I think it's too facile, a bit too glib.'

'To a degree,' he concurred. 'However, what you said about my not sharing was accurate and, with hindsight, I suspect it was the major factor in why none of my liaisons ever managed to get beyond first base. Of course, there were the occasions when I picked up vibrations of entrapment and shipped out, though——'

'You're anti-marriage because your parents' marriage failed?' Sian cut in.

'I was anti-marriage because I had a deep-rooted resistance to allowing what I thought had happened to my father happening to me,' Leith replied. 'But mostly my liaisons never stood a chance, because I never gave anything to them. From my side there was minimal emotional input and nothing by way of commitment, which could have something to do with my dragging the concepts of childhood with me, and thus doing a good job of convincing myself that women equalled getting hurt. How's that for self-analysis?' he demanded.

'Neat. Real neat.' She reached forward to put her empty glass on the table. 'And so you invariably became dissatisfied?'

'Yes.' Leith frowned. 'But it was different with you. Although for months our relationship was platonic, in every other way it was immensely satisfying. I think the fact that we were together because we were working together helped.'

'You mean you didn't see me as a girlfriend?'

'Not initially.'

Sian slid him a look. 'Why? Wasn't I well-dressed enough?'

'You dressed fine.' Leith gave a theatrical groan. 'The sight of your perky little bottom in those trousers of yours made my loins stir every time—and still does.'

'That's why you called me smarty-pants?' she asked, surprised.

'And because you're the brightest girl I've ever met. The sexual attraction was strong from the start and when I did eventually get around to kissing you it—well, it possessed all the whump, all the magic of a very first kiss. From then on, I didn't seem to have a will of my own and, even though I knew that in making love there was a risk of destroying everything between us, I couldn't help myself. When I awoke the morning after and saw you lying beside me—so trusting, so peaceful—I felt an enormous surge of happiness.' His tongue wetted his lips. 'But the next minute it was gloom and doom.'

'You didn't consider our night together offered any potential?' Sian asked, aware of a sneaky surge of happiness herself.

'On the contrary, I thought it possessed wonderful potential. I knew we had friendship with a strong fanciability factor, which is the best possible start, and yet I couldn't bring myself to trust my judgement.' Leith grimaced. 'One half of me was saying I must give us a chance, while the other half was floating above yelling that we'd never last and so I should cut loose now and limit the damage.'

'And in deciding to cut loose you hadn't reckoned on my arguing?'

'Not the way you did, and it got me so agitated, so mixed up. I was barely through the door before I started to think that maybe we could work something out—but I'd blown it!' Leith sank his head into his hands. 'An hour later my thoughts had crystallised and I knew I'd made a dreadful mistake. I felt like death and so *guilty*,' he said, his voice muffled. 'I decided I must throw myself on your mercy and beg forgiveness—do *anything* it took to get us back together again—but next I found things had been blown with my mother, too, and then I walked under the truck.' His eyes met hers. 'Was that some day!'

'And not much later you were doing your utmost to banish me,' she said, and was unable to disguise her hurt.

He moved closer along the couch. 'Sian, it was the desperate act of a desperate man, but I had to try. I knew you felt something for me and yet I couldn't let you tie yourself to a cripple, and that's what might have happened, isn't it?' he demanded. 'If I'd confessed my true feelings you'd have been tempted to throw in your lot with me?'

She frowned, acknowledging that he was right and yet unsure about giving too much away. 'Possibly.'

'But I wasn't prepared for you to restrict your life on my account.'

'Shouldn't that have been my decision?' Sian enquired.

'Could be, though it's hypothetical now— thank goodness.'

'You were horribly aggressive,' she recalled.

'Please accept my apology.' Leith cast her a look. 'Later, when I talked about how my father had rid himself of my mother, as I said, I was all too aware of parallels and I wanted to explain but——'

Sian shook her head. 'There aren't any parallels,' she said, her voice strong and sure. 'You were trying to send me away for my sake. He sent her away for his.'

'Thanks. Believe me, it was the first time I'd been such a——' he smiled '—slimeball? The first time I needed to be.'

'No one else ever dug in her heels and insisted on staying?'

'No. Some weren't too pleased to be shown the door, but it wasn't just me who was aware of the gap, you know.' Leith took hold of her hand, lacing his fingers with hers. 'You've logged a long list of firsts. You were the first so-called "reject" to argue so vociferously, you're my first female friend, and you're the first woman I've ever fallen head over heels in love with.'

Sian felt a billowing of joy. 'I am?'

'You are.' He raised her hand to his lips. 'I love you,' Leith said softly.

She had never imagined she would hear him say those words, and now her heart spilled over with happiness and she started to cry.

'Will we need to wait another thirty minutes until you stop?' he asked, drawing her into his arms.

'No,' she gasped.

He kissed her brow. 'That's a relief, because when you're ready there's another first to come.'

Sian took the handkerchief he had pulled from his pocket and wiped her cheeks. 'Go on,' she said, sniffing.

'You're the first person I've ever wanted to live with, and love, forever,' Leith said. 'Will you marry me?'

'Yes, please. And I love you, too,' she added fervently.

'I know.'

'You know when I hate you. You know when I love you. Grief, but you're smug,' she protested.

Leith grinned. 'Aren't I?'

His arms tightened around her and he began to kiss her with warm, eager, loving kisses. Mouth to mouth they clung, until Sian felt a fire begin to glow, starting deep inside and spreading, spreading, until its sensual flames were licking all over her.

'Leith, what about your ribs?' she protested, when he drew her upright and led her into the bedroom. 'And your legs? Are you——?'

'I'm in terrific shape,' he murmured, pulling her down with him on to the bed. His fingers came to the buttons on her shirt and the zip on her jeans, and he undressed her. 'But even if I'd been broken into a hundred pieces and was fastened together with piano wire, I'd still make love to you.'

'You're sure?' she murmured.

'Sian, I'm positive about *everything* with us.'

His touch was gentle, his kisses tender, and as he reverently demonstrated his love for her—with his hands, his lips, his body—Sian became aware of an almost spiritual dimension. She had heard about the holy nature of sex, but this was the first time she had known the caress of skin on skin to inspire such a soaring of the soul. This was the first time she had experienced such a yearning. Tranquillity was all around, and yet the air ebbed and flowed with emotion, with *love*. She revelled in their intimacy, in the leisurely trace of his lips across her body, in the trail of his tongue around her mouth. The boundaries of her passion were being pushed outwards, and she was aware of arriving at a new and exhilarating state of consciousness.

Sian moved beneath him, delighting in the weight of his body on hers. Her fingers roamed across his back and his shoulders, their tips absorbing the smoothness of his skin and the firm muscles beneath. The scent of him reached into her subconscious. The power of him ran in her veins. Clasping his head, she opened her mouth against his and kissed him with a desire which was fast spinning out of control. Leith's breathing quickened, he gave a low moan, and she knew he, too, could wait no longer.

As his thighs ground into hers, her womb pulsated and contracted. Together they clung, dissolving into each other until Sian did not know where he ended and she began—and they became one.

'About getting married,' she said, a long time later.

Leith stopped stroking the red-gold hair which was tousled across the pillow. 'You have opinions on the subject?' He groaned. 'I should have known.'

'There are just two things I'd like to discuss, and the first is your grandmother. I hope you're intending to invite her to the wedding?'

'You bet I am, and along with the invitation I'll be sending her a plane ticket, plus tickets for my uncles and aunts. We'll go and see her tomorrow, and tell her. Satisfied?'

Sian nodded. 'Satisfied.'

'I also want to raise the idea of her moving to a better house. My father left me a fair amount of cash and I'd like to use it to make life more comfortable for her—if you're agreeable?'

'Completely.' She grinned. 'Though your father wouldn't be.'

'He'd go berserk,' Leith agreed, 'but I can't help that. I need to make some kind of compensation for what he did. What's the second thing you want to discuss?' he queried.

Sian's eyes sparkled. 'Your shirts—the ironing thereof.'

He released a long-drawn-out sigh. 'I'll do them.'

'You will?'

'I'll do anything it takes to ensure that when I wake up every morning for the rest of my life, you'll be there,' Leith vowed. 'And if I don't have time—well, a creased shirt is neither here nor there.'

'You could be too busy working wonders with fillet steak to iron?' she enquired.

'I could be too busy working wonders with my wife.' His arm closed around her and he pressed his lips to her brow. 'What do you think?'

Sian's mouth created a luscious smile. 'I think that priorities are priorities,' she said.

my VALENTINE 1992

Celebrate the most romantic day of the year with
MY VALENTINE 1992—a sexy new collection of four
romantic stories written by our famous Temptation
authors:

> GINA WILKENS
> KRISTINE ROLOFSON
> JOANN ROSS
> VICKI LEWIS THOMPSON

My Valentine 1992—an exquisite escape into a romantic
and sensuous world.

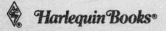

Harlequin Books®

VAL-92

HARLEQUIN
PROUDLY PRESENTS
A DAZZLING NEW CONCEPT IN ROMANCE FICTION

One small town—twelve terrific love stories

Welcome to Tyler, Wisconsin—a town full of people
you'll enjoy getting to know, memorable friends and
unforgettable lovers, and a long-buried secret that
lurks beneath its serene surface....

JOIN US FOR A YEAR IN THE LIFE OF TYLER

Each book set in Tyler is a self-contained love story;
together, the twelve novels stitch the fabric of a
community.

LOSE YOUR HEART TO TYLER!

The excitement begins in March 1992, with
WHIRLWIND, by Nancy Martin. When lively, brash
Liza Baron arrives home unexpectedly, she moves
into the old family lodge, where the silent and
mysterious Cliff Forrester has been living in seclusion
for years....

WATCH FOR ALL TWELVE BOOKS
OF THE TYLER SERIES
Available wherever Harlequin books are sold

TYLER-G

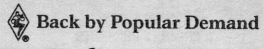

Back by Popular Demand

A romantic tour of America through fifty favorite
Harlequin Presents, each set in a different state
researched by Janet and her husband, Bill. A journey
of a lifetime in one cherished collection.

In January, don't miss the exciting states featured in:

Title #23 MINNESOTA
Giant of Mesabi

#24 MISSISSIPPI
A Tradition of Pride

Available wherever
Harlequin books are sold.

JD-JAN